THE BEACHSIDE INN

MARIGOLD ISLAND BOOK ONE

FIONA BAKER

CHAPTER ONE

Lydia's view from the ferry couldn't have been better. The pale blue sky blended in with the rich blue-green water at the horizon, a line that was only broken by the occasional island or two. It was unseasonably warm for mid-March, at least by southern Massachusetts' standards, so she could stand out on the deck to fully enjoy it.

The wind picked up a few strands of her long brunette hair, whipping them around her face. She tucked them behind her ear as the ferry moved along at a steady clip toward her destination—Marigold Island.

She hadn't been there in years, but something in her gut was telling her it was time to go back. She wasn't sure what had caused that feeling, but then again, there was a lot she was unsure of these days.

One thing she did know was that she missed her daughter, Holly. Lydia dug her phone out of her purse and scrolled through her recent contacts before pressing the *call* button.

"Hey, Mom," Holly said, sounding out of breath. "Give me a second—I'm just getting in from class, and it's snowing like crazy. What's up? How are you?"

"Just wanted to say hi. I missed you." Lydia paused, hearing the noise of Holly's dorm hallway in the background. "It's still snowing? Are you warm enough?"

"It's Syracuse—snow's the rule, not the exception until like, June. People are going to break out their shorts the moment the temperatures rise above freezing. And yes, I'm toasty. I'm wearing about seventy layers right now, and they're a pain to take off." Holly snorted. "Also, you did that thing again."

"What thing?"

"The thing where I ask you how you are, and you don't give me an answer," Holly said.

Lydia sighed and leaned against the ferry's railing, listening to her daughter kick off her boots. With the background noise of other students now muffled behind the dorm room door, the truth of Holly's words could fully sink in.

"Well, I'm fine." Lydia managed to keep the uncertainty out of her voice.

"Just fine?"

"Which one of us is the mom here?" Lydia tried to laugh to lighten the mood, but she knew she failed. She could practically see Holly's dark eyebrows pulling together in a frown, just like her father's used to.

"Seriously, though. I'm worried." Holly's voice got quieter. "I just want you to be happy again. It's been a year..."

She didn't have to finish that sentence, because both of them were constantly aware of the gap in their lives. Lydia could hardly believe it had been a year since her husband Paul's death. It felt like ages had passed.

"I know, sweetheart. I'm happy." The words didn't feel quite right on Lydia's tongue. "And visiting Aunt Millie will perk me up even more."

Lydia heard more commotion on Holly's side, probably from her roommate Valerie.

"Okay, if you say so." Holly's deep sigh made her seem much older than her nineteen years. "Hey, I gotta go—Annie and I are going to grab something to eat before the weather gets worse. Promise to give Aunt Millie a hug for me, okay?"

"I promise. Love you. Bye."

"Love you too, Mom."

Lydia ended the call and tucked her phone back into her purse. As she did, her fingers almost automatically reached for the last letter Paul had ever written her, which she kept with her at all times. She pulled it out and turned against the wind, just in case the breeze picked up and tried to tug the paper from her grasp.

The ink was starting to fade already, even though Paul had used one of his favorite pens that seemed to leave twice the amount of ink a regular pen would. His words had smudged a little more than usual, making his familiar blocky handwriting skewed. Cancer had stolen all of his strength, so even writing a letter was harder for him at the end.

Lyds,

Remember that first letter I gave you, way back when we first started dating? I sweated over that thing for about a week before I dared to slip it into your locker. I wanted to impress you so badly, but I didn't know what to write.

But this one is even harder to get down on paper—I don't think I could ever put how much I love you into words. Every single day, even the worst ones, got a little better when I got to be with you. I wish I could be there for everything, even your terrible coffee (okay, fine, it's an acquired taste). I want to see Holly continue to blossom, and I want to take that trip to New Zealand to see all those sheep and convince you to bungee jump. All of those things and more.

I can't, but I can leave you with this:

Don't let your life stop when I'm gone. Keep going and find happiness, because you deserve it. You're too incredible to stay at home, not sharing yourself with the world.

And do something that scares you. Maybe not right away, but don't wait too long. Just trust me on this.

Love you more than I can say,

Paul

Lydia folded the paper gently and made sure it was safely inside her purse before she turned back to look at the water stretched out before her.

The part that read *do something that scares you* always stood out to her. She hadn't known how scary and uncertain doing just about anything would feel without Paul, but she knew that wasn't the kind of fear that he was talking about. He wanted her to do something big.

The problem was, she had no idea what that could be.

She knew she was barely fulfilling his first final wish. She hadn't let her life stop entirely after his passing—she still kept up with things at home and went to her job at the travel agency where she'd worked for years. She even went to the gym from time to time. But that was about it: home, work, home again, with calls with Holly in between. Every day, stuck in a loop she didn't know how to get out of.

Maybe this trip is the first step to moving on, Lydia thought as the boat slowed to dock in the harbor.

Lydia got off the ferry and made her way up the path toward the parking lot where she was going to meet Millie. Lydia found her aunt chatting with a woman pushing a stroller and waved. Millie's face lit up, and she excused herself from her conversation after giving the woman she had been talking to a quick hug.

Lydia couldn't help but smile. Millie was a hugger for sure.

Millie waved to someone else before she crossed the street to greet Lydia. Was it possible for one woman to know all ten thousand people living on Marigold Island? It sure felt like Millie did.

"Lydia!" Millie said, opening her arms. "I've missed you so much!"

Lydia laughed and stepped into Millie's warm hug. "I missed you too. You look great!"

Millie really did. She was in her mid-sixties, but her energy and warmth made her seem a decade younger. Her dark gray hair tumbled down her shoulders as it always had. Lydia had never known Millie without some grays in her hair and always thought it was beautiful.

Lydia hadn't realized how much she missed Millie. Had the last time they'd seen each other been at Paul's funeral? Now that she thought about it, she realized it had been, and it'd been even longer since Lydia had visited Millie on the island. Millie was Lydia's only living family now besides Holly, since her parents had died in an accident nine years ago. Lydia needed to take every chance to visit.

"You look wonderful too." Millie squeezed both of Lydia's shoulders and looked her over. "Shall we head out? I'm sure you're hungry."

Lydia adored Millie's cooking. "I definitely am. I haven't eaten a proper meal all day—just something on the go."

They hopped into Millie's car and drove off. One of Lydia's favorite things about Marigold Island was how easy it was to get around, especially in comparison to Boston. There wasn't much traffic, and no truck horns blared. The busiest road ran straight through the middle of town, which was lined with adorable shops.

"How was the trip over? You picked a great day to arrive," Millie said, glancing over at Lydia in the passenger seat.

Lydia pressed her hands to her cheeks, which were slightly chilled from the wind. "It was nice. It feels good to get away for once. I swear, I tell my clients at the travel agency that they should visit Marigold all the time, but I never take my own advice."

Lydia grinned as she saw the shops on Main Street come into view in the distance. The downtown area of the island town was small, but it was packed full of locally owned restaurants, bars, and a variety of shops.

"For a travel agent, it seems like you don't do much traveling yourself." Millie cocked an eyebrow as she slowed at a stop sign and let someone else pass through the intersection first.

"I know." Lydia sighed. "It's just been at the bottom of my priority list."

"What's been at the top?"

"Just... life, I suppose. Work has been busy, especially with the summer coming up soon. I've been keeping in touch with Holly a lot. She's doing great. She's finally landed on being an education major."

Lydia saw Millie nod out of the corner of her eye. Both of them knew what Lydia wasn't mentioning. Lydia was grateful that her aunt knew when to press something and when to back off.

Lydia perked up again when The Sweet Creamery came into view. A few families were sitting out front enjoying their ice cream, even though it was still a little cold for it.

"I got us a pint of red velvet cake ice cream for after dinner," Millie said with a grin when she saw where Lydia was looking.

"That's exactly why you're the best."

The Sweet Creamery's ice cream blew all the ice cream shops in Boston out of the water. Part of it was the charm of the place—it was an old-fashioned ice cream parlor that had been updated with bright lights and a counter where people could sit and enjoy their treats. But the other part was just how delicious every flavor was, even the ones that Lydia didn't think she'd enjoy, like rosewater and pistachio.

The other shops on the street were equally

charming, their wood siding painted in light, beachy colors. There was Darcy's Crafts, which hosted a weekly "wine and paint" night that Lydia had been to once before, and Franklin's Hardware, which had been there for as long as she could remember. There were also some newer businesses, like a pet supply store and a surf shop.

They passed from the middle of town toward the more residential half, the shops giving way to well-manicured streets and the occasional glimpse of the ocean in the distance. Lydia leaned against the window, taking in the way the afternoon light filtered through the trees. She could smell the ocean, even from the car. In Marigold, it always felt like you were a quick walk from the water, no matter where you were in town.

A few minutes later, Millie pulled onto her street. None of the houses looked exactly alike, but most of them were New England style cottages. Millie's was toward the end of the road. Even though her home was small, it radiated warmth just like its owner did. Millie loved to garden, so her tiny front yard looked lush and alive despite it only being early spring. She'd painted her door magenta, and the color really popped against the white of the rest of the exterior and the dark blue of the roof.

It was just as cozy on the inside, somehow managing to be filled with all sorts of knick-knacks and pieces of art without seeming cluttered, even in the tight space. The savory smell of Millie's famous slow-cooked pot roast filled the air, making Lydia's stomach growl loudly. The two women laughed as Lydia put her bag down.

"Come on into the kitchen," Millie said with a wave. "I've got to put the finishing touches on dinner."

The two women worked together to finish the meal prep, which only took a few minutes. Then Lydia helped Millie bring all the food to the table. In addition to the pot roast, Millie had made mashed potatoes that were lighter and fluffier than Lydia thought possible and a simple salad to balance out the heaviness of the rest of the meal.

"We both deserve a little wine, don't you think?" Millie raised a bottle of red wine as they settled in at the table—a Pedroncelli zinfandel. Her taste in wine was just as good as her cooking.

"Of course we do." Lydia smiled and pushed her wine glass toward Millie.

"Cheers to our reunion," Millie said, raising her glass.

"I'll drink to that." Lydia gently tapped her glass

against Millie's and took a sip. The wine was perfect, ever so slightly dry without overpowering all the other subtle fruity notes.

The two women dug into their food, only pausing to murmur about how delicious it all was. Once both of them got enough food in their bellies, they caught up with each other, keeping the conversation light. Lydia told her all about Holly and her newly chosen education major, as well as a few updates on how things were going at the travel agency where she worked.

Millie, as always, was involved in a number of projects and events around town. There was a festival coming up in the summer, a parade, a new community mural down near the beach, and a fundraiser for revitalizing one of the old piers. It was so vastly different from life in Boston that it almost felt like Lydia had traveled to another planet instead of another state. Marigold Island was truly a community—people leaned on each other and took care of each other in a way that you just couldn't find in the city.

"Mmm, I can't believe how good this is. It's even better than I remember," Lydia said as she took her first bite of red velvet ice cream not long after they'd finished their main meal. Her eyes fluttered closed so she could focus entirely on the sweetness of the creamy ice cream and the bits of red velvet cake.

Millie nodded. "The Sweet Creamery is going to have an ice cream party when summer comes. I wish you could be here for it."

"Same," Lydia said. "Maybe I'll make another quick trip up for it."

"Maybe."

Lydia glanced at Millie, knowing how much meaning was packed into that "maybe." Millie always wanted her to stay longer, but in the past, Lydia had always had an excuse. She had her job and Holly, plenty of reasons to hurry back to Boston.

But as she thought of the quiet, cozy island around them, so different from the constant hum of activity back home, Lydia wished she could stay a little longer, too.

CHAPTER TWO

Would Angela ever have a morning that wasn't pure chaos?

Probably not.

Her lips twisted wryly at the thought as she bustled around her house. There were pants on the kitchen floor, keys in the bathroom, books in the hallway, and paint color swatches in the cabinet next to the cereal.

She swore that her home had been in its proper order the night before. Now she was wondering if that had all been a hallucination.

Trying to get her six-year-old son, Jake, ready for school was a balancing act that she and her husband Scott had yet to perfect. She now understood the phrase, "it's like herding cats," more than she'd ever thought she would. Jake seemed like he could be everywhere at once, a skill Angela wished she had too.

"Mommy?" Jake asked, coming to a skidding stop in his socks in front of the open door to the bathroom.

"Yes, sweetheart?"

Angela stopped putting on her makeup. Ever since she'd had Jake, she'd perfected a fast, minimal routine that didn't require much precision—she could just rub tinted creams onto her face, do her hair in a few steps, and end up looking mostly awake and presentable. Even her wardrobe was set up so that she could look put together just by grabbing a random pair of pants and a blouse.

"Daddy says I can't bring cookies for lunch. Can I bring cookies for lunch?" Jake's big blue eyes, which looked like mirrors of hers, were wide and pleading. "Please?"

"What else is Daddy helping you pack?"

She glanced at herself in the mirror, then at the clock on the counter. They were already running behind. How was that possible? Everyone had gotten up early this morning. She felt like time always went twice as fast when she wanted it to slow down.

"Um... food." Jake shifted from foot to foot. "But I just want cookies."

Angela quickly tied her honey-blonde hair back into its usual bun—long gone were the days when she spent fifteen whole minutes styling just her hair —and ushered her son down the hallway to the kitchen.

"We can't just do cookies. We have to have some regular food too," she said. "Scott, what are you packing?"

Her husband was carefully cutting a sandwich into four squares the way Jake liked it. He was already dressed for work, his brown hair disheveled despite his face being clean-shaven. He hadn't been clean-shaven in a while, but she liked it. In the thirteen years they'd been together, he usually had stubble or even a beard.

"His regular stuff—sandwich, baby carrots, and one little pack of cookies." Scott looked down at his son, who was skipping across the open floor plan from the living room to the kitchen and back. "The cookies will be a special treat, bud. They won't feel special if you *only* have cookies."

"Mmmm..." Jake looked between his parents. "Okay!"

Angela and Scott exchanged relieved looks. Jake

had enough energy to power half of Philadelphia, but thankfully, he was also a very agreeable kid. He always had been.

"Breakfast!" Angela said, snapping her fingers. "We should probably do that, huh?"

She quickly threw together some toast and eggs for Jake and poured herself some coffee in a to-go thermos. She had a granola bar in her purse to scarf down on her commute and probably had yogurt in the office fridge.

As Jake ate, she checked over the big calendar on the fridge as well as her work calendar on her phone to make sure everything was in order. Thankfully, Friday was takeout night so she wouldn't have to cook anything, but she also had a packed day between meetings with clients and with the people on her team. Takeout, which was probably going to be pizza, would likely be her only meal eaten while sitting down.

So, it was like most weekdays. At least the weekend was coming up.

Scott hurried Jake through the rest of breakfast and helped him find his socks while Angela checked through her son's backpack to make sure he had everything he needed. She grabbed her coffee, her bag, and Jake's lunch box, and managed to give Scott a kiss on the cheek before heading out. She and Jake made it to the school bus just in the nick of time.

All-in-all, Angela considered this morning a success.

She made it to the office with three whole minutes to gather her wits before a video conference call with a client. Some days, she wanted an hour to just breathe, but she loved her work. She was an interior designer and got to help people put together homes and offices that they loved walking into every day. What could be better than that?

The video call went well and miraculously ended fifteen minutes early, giving Angela more time to eat her yogurt and prepare for her next meeting. She plopped down at her desk and reached for a post-it before a realization hit her: she'd forgotten a binder filled with paint and fabric swatches at home, and she needed it for this next meeting. She knew exactly where it was—tucked away on the couch where she'd fallen asleep watching TV the night before.

At least she had time to run home and get it. She told her assistant that she'd be right back and rushed out. Her commute was usually ten minutes each way if she didn't have to drop Jake off at the bus stop, so she had just enough time to grab the binder and get back on time.

What a stroke of luck, she thought, digging her keys out of her purse. She almost never got breaks in the day like this and usually never forgot anything so important at home.

Angela heard music the second she opened the door, and her brows furrowed. Had Scott left it on? It was coming from the bedroom. She made her way toward their bedroom, opening her mouth to call out to him.

But she stopped dead in the doorway as she got a look inside the room.

Scott was in bed, tucked under the covers, and some woman she didn't recognize was wearing *her* bathrobe as if she had the right to. All three of them stared at each other for several long beats, the scenario made even stranger by some 90s dance song Angela vaguely remembered playing in the background.

Shock made it impossible to speak. As she gaped at Scott and the other woman in the bedroom, Angela searched her memories, trying to pinpoint where she'd seen this woman before.

College? No, the woman was younger than both her and Scott by at least five or six years.

Jake's school? A yoga class?

Then recognition clicked in—she was one of Scott's coworkers. Her name started with an S or an R. Angela had liked her when they'd met once at a barbecue. Now, her opinion had obviously taken a complete turn for the worse.

"Um... I'll leave," the woman murmured, grabbing her clothes and slipping quickly into the bathroom. Into *Angela's* bathroom. This woman shouldn't have been within a hundred yards of their home.

Angela stood there, feeling so boneless that she was surprised she was still standing. Scott couldn't meet her gaze, not that she wanted to look at him. The woman emerged from the bathroom fully dressed and rushed out, not saying a word. The front door clicked behind her.

Scott pressed the heels of his hands to his eyes and sighed.

"Angela..."

"Who on earth was that, Scott? Isn't she one of your coworkers?" Angela asked, finally lurching out of her stasis. She strode quickly into the bedroom and turned off the music. "Why was she in our house wearing my bathrobe?"

"Why don't you sit down, and we can talk about it?"

"I'm not sitting down on this bed after what's happened here." Angela stalked back out into the hallway, anger rising up to replace the numb shock. "We're going to the dining room."

Scott didn't protest. Angela found the binder she had left behind on the couch, where she thought she'd left it, and tucked it under her arm. She wondered what would have happened if she hadn't heard the music. She could have walked in, gotten what she needed, and walked out without even knowing what Scott was up to.

Would that have been any better? Walking into her home where her husband was cheating on her and leaving in a state of blissful ignorance?

She wasn't sure. She still felt like she was watching someone *else's* life get shaken up and turned completely on its side—not her own.

Angela sat down at the dining room table, which she'd gotten for a bargain at an antiques sale and refinished herself. Just the night before, they'd had a nice meal at this table, sitting together as a family. Scott had told her and Jake about a street magician he'd seen on his lunch break, making Jake laugh. Had Scott met up with that woman yesterday too?

Angela looked at herself in the mirror she'd placed on one side of the room to open it up. She loved the mirror, but wasn't sure about the reflection she saw anymore. She felt small and unattractive in a way that she never had before. The fine lines around her eyes and mouth suddenly felt like big wrinkles, and she questioned whether the long-sleeved silk blouse she had on looked dowdy or not.

She shook her head and looked back down at the binder. Those thoughts weren't helping. And it wasn't *her* fault that Scott had cheated on her. The blame for that rested entirely on him.

Finally, Scott made his way into the dining room wearing a t-shirt and jeans. He sat on the opposite side of the table from her, accurately sensing that she didn't want him to come close to her at the moment.

He ran a hand through his hair and sighed, still not meeting her gaze for an uncomfortably long time.

"Ange..." Scott finally looked at her. "I'm sorry. This was just a lapse in judgment. Well, two lapses—"

"You've slept with her more than once?" Angela was surprised she didn't scream the words, even though she wanted to.

"This was only the second time. I promise. She's a coworker of mine." Scott rested his forearms on the table. "I know you probably won't believe me, but I really do want to be with you. It's just... it's complicated."

"Complicated. Okay."

"I've been in a rough place lately, feeling a little stuck. I should've talked to you about it, and we could've found a way through it together. But instead, I messed up by letting things develop between me and Sadie—things that never should've happened. I feel like the biggest jerk in the world. You've been nothing but good to me in all the years we've been together, and I failed you."

He sounded and looked sincere, but now Angela didn't trust his word in the slightest. Scott, the man she'd been in love with for over a decade, now looked like a complete stranger. Where was the man who had swept her off her feet all those years ago? The man who was always there to make her feel better when she was down on herself or unsure? Suddenly, she couldn't stand to be in the same room as him.

She gathered her purse and the binder she'd come home for, standing up.

"Where are you going?" Scott scrambled to his feet too.

"Back to work. I don't know what else to do, but I

know that I don't want to be here with you right now. And I'm super late for this meeting."

Angela swallowed the lump in her throat. She was surprised she wasn't crying, but she was certain that would come later. Right now, she was still reeling from what she'd discovered, her emotions too unsettled to process any of them completely.

"Can we talk about it later tonight?" Scott asked.

Angela looked at him, trying to understand what she was feeling. What *he* was feeling.

"No. I need space, okay? I think you should stay somewhere else tonight. I'll tell Jake that you had to go on an unexpected business trip."

With that, Angela stepped out of their home and shut the door behind her. She managed to keep it together until she got to her car, where the sadness finally washed over her like a tidal wave.

She took several deep breaths, then let herself burst into tears.

* * *

"Look at that bird!" Jake said, pointing at a seagull sitting on the dock where their ferry had just pulled into Marigold Island. "And that one! He's floating!"

"Pretty cool, huh? You don't see those back

home," Angela said with a surprising amount of pep, given the circumstances.

After learning about Scott's infidelity, she couldn't stand to be at home. There were too many memories there for her to think clearly. If she looked at their bathroom, all she could think of was that woman putting on her bathrobe in there. If she looked at the dining room table, the memories of confronting Scott came rushing up.

Everything in the house screamed at her to make a rash decision, which was the last thing she needed to do. So, she'd decided to take Jake and stay with her parents for a few days to clear her head. Marigold Island was the perfect place to find peace. The pace was slower, and the people were nicer. Even the air felt better in her lungs. She always came back to Marigold when she needed to think.

Her parents, Phoebe and Mitch, lived in a beautiful cottage not far from the water, tucked into a grove of old trees that hadn't quite recovered from winter yet. When the cab dropped her and Jake off, Angela saw two additional cars in the driveway. They belonged to her younger brother and sister, Travis and Brooke.

Jake darted up the driveway toward the front door just as it opened.

"Grammy!" Jake said, throwing his arms around his grandmother's waist.

"Who is this big boy? I missed you, Jake!" Phoebe laughed and managed to ruffle Jake's hair before he ran inside toward the other happy voices Angela heard. "He's grown so much."

"He has. It feels like I buy him new shoes every other week," Angela said, dragging their suitcases up the paved driveway.

"Come here, Angie." Phoebe opened her arms, her expression slightly concerned.

Angela wrapped her arms around her mother and squeezed. The familiar scent of her mother's gardenia perfume was an instant comfort, as was the hug. Angela couldn't count the number of times she'd hugged her mom just like this or asked for advice when things got hard. When Angela had called to tell Phoebe what happened with Scott, Phoebe had known exactly what to say to help her get through the night.

"Where's my Angela?" Mitch's voice boomed over the sound of Jake's excited giggling and her siblings' chatter.

"Hey, Dad."

Angela walked into her father's hug, which was just as comforting as her mother's. Mitch had been a firefighter before he retired, but he still worked out regularly as if he had to go into the station the next day. His strength made Angela feel like he was literally holding her up.

"Let me get your things. You can head on inside," Mitch said, gently guiding her in.

Angela stepped into the house and inhaled deeply. Phoebe had something that smelled divine in the oven, and the scent floated through the house. Angela had helped decorate the space a few years ago, and she was happy to see a few well-placed updates in the classic beach cottage decor. The whole house was cozy, inviting, and well-loved.

Angela spotted Travis and Brooke in the living room with Jake. Travis looked more and more like their father every day, especially when he smiled, but his sandy brown hair was thick and free of any gray strands. Brooke looked more like Angela and Phoebe, but her hair was a paler blonde than Angela's. It was the kind of gorgeous, beachy color that Angela's friends back in Philadelphia would have paid good money to get from the salon.

Travis pulled his older sister into a big bear hug before Brooke could say hello, lifting Angela into the air a few inches. The very slight softness she used to feel when she hugged him had been replaced with more warm, solid muscle.

"Wow, did you quit the police force just to work out?" Angela asked, looking up at Travis when he released her. She still couldn't get over how tall he was, even though he had been this height since he was a teenager. "What's the deal?"

"Nope." Travis's grin widened. "A new gym opened up on the far side of the island, so I've been going there after my shift ends several times a week."

"I'm gonna be as big and strong as Uncle Travis one day," Jake said, looking up at his uncle with a determined gleam in his eyes.

"You will if you eat your vegetables and go to bed on time like I do." Travis rested his hand on Jake's head. Then he chuckled. "Brooke's making the first part harder and harder, even for me. I'm probably thirty percent butter now."

"I can't eat all the things I bake by myself!" Brooke gently elbowed Travis aside so she could finally hug Angela. "Missed you, Ange."

"Missed you too." Angela gave her little sister one more squeeze before letting her go. "You're still working on your baking?"

"Yep. I go through flour like crazy." Brooke

squeezed her sister's arms, waggling her eyebrows. "I made Oreo pie for dessert."

"Perfect. I need some comfort food." Angela glanced down at Jake, who was still oblivious to why they had actually come to visit his grandparents, aunt, and uncle. "Talk later?"

"Of course." Brooke nodded, knowing exactly what Angela needed.

"Everyone come to the table. The food's ready," Mitch called.

He didn't have to ask twice. Phoebe had pulled out all the stops for Angela and Jake's arrival—there was roasted chicken with perfectly crispy skin, au gratin potatoes, green beans, macaroni and cheese, and freshly baked rolls. And of course, there was wine. The perfect kind of home cooking, shared with the people she loved.

Angela could tell her family was keeping the conversation light and uplifting for her sake, which she appreciated. Even though Marigold was small and not as "exciting" as the big city, everyone had funny or outrageous stories to tell.

Between the food, the warm laughter they shared, and the wine, Angela was well on her way to feeling... not great, but definitely less awful. She'd missed this. For once, she didn't have anywhere to rush to or any fires to put out. She didn't even have to get up fifty times during the meal to get something for Jake, because Mitch or Phoebe would volunteer to do it for her. Maybe she needed more of this in her life.

More family. More time. More *space*.

After dinner, Jake dragged his grandparents and uncle outside to play while Angela and Brooke had a little extra pie and watched them from the back porch. The large porch was a newer addition to their parents' house, and it had gotten a lot of use already. Mitch's grill was on one side, and the cozy chairs where Angela and Brooke sat were on the other, overlooking the fenced-in backyard. They weren't very close to the beach, but the air still had the crisp, clean scent of the woods that spread out beyond the line of the fence.

The two sisters sat in silence for a few moments. Brooke was seven years younger than Angela, but she had matured enough to understand her sister's need for quiet sometimes. Angela appreciated her family's attempts at distracting her, but now she needed to think a little. Eventually, Angela spoke up.

"I'm going to ask Scott for a divorce."

"Yeah?" Brooke's eyebrows went up. "You've already made up your mind?"

Angela watched Travis pick up Jake, both of them laughing as her brother spun the little boy around on his shoulders.

"Yeah. I think it's time to start over altogether. I guess this is whole situation is making me realize just how frazzled I am all the time. This is the first time I've eaten dinner without rushing to do the next thing on my to-do list. Maybe if I wasn't stretched so thin, I would have noticed something was up sooner."

Even though Scott had said that he'd only slipped up twice, Angela couldn't stop thinking about when his dissatisfaction with their marriage had started. Had it been years?

She'd thought she was paying attention. It hurt to realize that she'd missed something that now felt so obvious. Sometimes, he'd seemed to be a little too friendly with other women at parties, which she'd brushed off as him having a little too much wine, and recently, he'd started caring about his appearance more than he used to. Angela wanted to kick herself for not connecting the dots. Not seeing what was right in front of her face.

"Angie, don't blame yourself for what he did. He was hiding on purpose. He was sneaking around and cheating on you. Of *course* you didn't notice. You trusted him." Brooke put her empty dessert plate on the small table between them. "This is all on him. He's a jerk."

"I know. It's just hard." Angela sighed and polished off the last of her slice of Oreo pie. It was so good that it alone was making her feel less terrible. "I feel totally thrown off balance by all of this, like the rug got ripped out from under me. I feel unattractive and stupid."

"What? No! You aren't either of those things!" Brooke's blue eyes went wide. She shook her head emphatically, scowling. "And I wish I could call Scott to yell at him for making you feel like that."

Angela couldn't help but smile. Brooke was a sweet person, more prone to laughter than shouting —but she didn't like anyone messing with her family.

"I bet he wouldn't know what to do with himself."

"Oh, he wouldn't. And there wouldn't be much left of him after I got through with him." Brooke relaxed a little, looking back over at the yard. "But seriously, you deserve to feel good. You're an amazing woman, and you deserve to feel confident and happy—and a reset could be the thing to give you that."

"True." Angela shrugged, feeling a bit of optimism return to her spirit. "Why not now?"

"Yeah, why not?" Brooke smiled. "We'll all be here for you every step of the way."

Angela knew her family always had her back, but for some reason, hearing Brooke say it made a lump of emotion rise in her throat. She felt more grateful than ever to have people in her corner.

It wasn't going to be easy, but Angela had already built an amazing life once before. Now, she just had to do it again.

CHAPTER THREE

Breakfast at Phoebe and Mitch's house was so drastically different from the ones back in Philadelphia that Angela wondered if she was still dreaming. Jake's excited chatter was still the same, but nothing else was. She had gotten a surprising amount of sleep, she didn't feel the need to catapult herself into whatever needed to be done today, and it smelled like pancakes instead of whatever she or Scott had thrown together at the last minute.

Angela brushed her teeth and made herself somewhat presentable before heading downstairs and into the kitchen. Jake was standing on a chair next to his grandpa, stirring pancake batter in a huge bowl. Both Jake's and Mitch's pajamas were covered in flour, as if they'd missed the bowl on purpose.

Phoebe was flipping bacon on the griddle while nursing a cup of coffee.

"Mommy, we're making pancakes!" Jake looked up and pointed at the bowl proudly.

"I see that. What kind?" Angela made a beeline over to the coffee maker.

"Chocolate chip!"

Angela exchanged a glance with her mother as she poured a little cream, then a little coffee into her mug. Jake was hyper enough without a blast of sugar first thing in the morning—he was going to jump through the roof after eating those pancakes. Phoebe just laughed and put some bacon on a paper towel covered plate to drain.

"It's the weekend, and you're on vacation. What would a Saturday be like without a little sugar to start your day?" Phoebe said to her daughter, as if she'd read her mind.

Angela watched Jake carefully stir the chocolate chips into the batter like it was the biggest responsibility in the world, then smiled. Phoebe had a point. They usually only had chocolate chip pancakes on special occasions, but why not now? Here on Marigold, Jake had plenty of space to run around and work out his energy. They just had to step into the backyard instead of walking to the park.

Angela helped set the table while Jake and her parents finished making breakfast. By the time they settled down to eat, Angela's coffee had started to kick in. She doused her pancakes in syrup and butter. Mitch's pancakes were legendary in the family, and for good reason. Angela hummed with happiness when the sweetness of the fluffy pancakes spread across her tongue. It had been way too long since she'd had a breakfast like this.

Everyone seemed to agree, complimenting Jake on his skill with the chocolate chips and munching on crunchy strips of bacon.

"What do you want to do today, sweetheart?" Angela asked, wiping some stray syrup off one of Jake's cheeks as he swallowed a big bite.

He could eat a lot of pancakes for such a little guy. Then again, it felt like he grew another few inches from one day to the next, so he needed the fuel.

"We were thinking about taking him down to the beach," Mitch said before Jake could answer. Then he turned to his grandson. "One of my friends who lives down there has a new puppy, too, if you want to visit them."

Jake gasped. "Yes! I wanna go!"

Angela laughed. Jake *loved* dogs, but the idea of

juggling a rambunctious kid and an equally energetic dog was a daunting prospect. Plus, their home in Philly wasn't big enough for all three of them plus the bigger breeds that she, Scott, and Jake liked.

"We won't be going home with a brand new puppy, will we?" Angela asked, narrowing her eyes a little.

"No, of course not," Mitch said with a mischievous smile. Angela knew he would never go against her wishes on something like that, but he liked to tease.

"Take the day to yourself, honey." Phoebe patted her hand. "We'll have a fun day with Jake, and you can do what you need to do. Then we could do something fun for dinner. You want to help with dinner too, Jake?"

Jake nodded, stuffing more pancakes into his mouth.

"Thank you," Angela said, a strange blend of relief and anxiety filling her.

She really wanted a little time to herself. She needed the quiet and the space to think through her decision to file for divorce, but the thought of actually figuring things out was daunting. She'd have to find a lawyer and consider how everything would be split up between her and Scott—not to mention how Jake fit in.

Taking a walk would help her get her jumbled thoughts in order, especially with the beauty of the small island town all around her. It just wasn't the same as taking a walk in Philly, even though she lived in a walkable part of the city. Walking in Marigold was truly relaxing without all the honking cars and crowds of people.

They finished breakfast and got properly dressed, taking their time in a way that Angela rarely got to experience. Even Saturdays usually meant rushing around, taking Jake to activities or birthday parties. It was nice enough outside for Angela to get away with wearing a dark blue cable-knit sweater under a light jacket and her favorite jeans.

Phoebe, Mitch, and Jake were going to play in the backyard for a while, so Angela gave everyone hugs and kisses before heading out. One of the best parts about where her parents lived was how easy it was to get down to Main Street on foot. The neatly paved sidewalks were lined with trees and large houses, until those gave way to the businesses of the downtown area.

Angela noticed some new businesses right away, like Anchorhead Coffee and Darcy's Crafts. Both looked like they fit into the neighborhood despite being a little more modern in comparison to the other businesses on Main. She was surprised at how much Marigold was able to evolve while still maintaining the warm, cozy charm that made it special.

Angela meandered around, unsure of where to go. She popped into Darcy's Crafts to see if there was anything Jake would like to do and bought him a new set of markers. She treated herself to a latte at Anchorhead Coffee and sipped it as she sat down on a bench outside.

Leaning back a little, she wrapped both hands around her warm paper cup as she people-watched. Since it was Saturday, there were a lot of people out, wandering around and looking at what Marigold had to offer. There was a nip in the air, but many people were already starting to break out their lighter coats like she had.

Angela felt a bolt of recognition as she scanned the crowd. A brown-haired woman was walking across the street, glancing at her phone. It'd been years since Angela had seen her, but she'd recognize her old friend Lydia Walker anywhere. They'd spent most of their summers together growing up, all the way through high school.

Whenever Lydia came to Marigold for the

summer, she, Angela, and their two other friends, Grace and Rachel, would spend almost every day together, and many nights, talking and sharing everything. They'd drifted apart in college despite their phone calls and letters, and eventually they fell out of touch when real life hit and jobs, kids, and spouses pulled them in different directions. Angela still got some updates from her parents about her old friends from time to time, but she regretted losing touch with the ladies.

The warm memories of their friendship were yet another reason why she loved Marigold so much.

"Lydia!" Angela hopped to her feet, nearly spilling the rest of her drink.

Lydia looked up, a confused expression on her face until she saw who was calling her name. Then, her eyes lit up.

"Angela?" Lydia finished crossing to Angela's side of the street and hurried down the sidewalk toward her. "Oh, wow! I can't believe it's you!"

The two women hugged each other tightly. Something about the hug made Angela feel like a teenager again without a care in the world.

"It's been so long." As Angela spoke, she studied her friend.

Lydia looked great—her brunette hair had some

reddish highlights and was cut just above her shoulders. She still had the same warm, gentle smile that Angela remembered.

Lydia nodded. "It really has!"

"Do you want to grab an early lunch or something? I'd love to catch up." Even though they hadn't spoken in a long while, Angela knew her friend would be the perfect person to help her decompress.

"Yes, I would love that!" Lydia squeezed Angela's upper arms before letting go. "There's a nice lunch place that opened up one street over not long ago. I've heard the sandwiches and salads are incredible."

Angela thought about the pancakes that had felt so filling not long ago. Now she found herself ready to eat again. Something about Marigold made her hungry—maybe because all the food was delicious, whether you were in someone's home or at a restaurant.

"That sounds perfect," she agreed.

The two women headed over to the restaurant, Brick and Barrel, and got a seat at a booth in the corner. They could see boats in the harbor far beyond the trees through one window, and bungalows and small businesses through the other. Angela checked over the menu, overwhelmed with the wide array of delicious choices. All of it sounded so good. Both she and Lydia went with the waiter's suggestion—lobster bisque.

"How long have you been in town?" Angela asked, sipping her water.

"I just got in yesterday."

"Ah, same with me and my son."

"Your husband didn't tag along?" Lydia frowned.

"Not this time, no. We're..." Angela didn't know how to broach the topic. Saying it out loud was still surreal. "I'm taking some time away from him." She grimaced. "I walked in on him with another woman."

"Oh Angie. I'm so, so sorry," Lydia said. Her eyes went from sad compassion to irritation. "God, I wish I could yell at him right now."

Angela managed to laugh. "That's exactly what my sister said. That's what I wanted to do when I found out, honestly. But it's better that I didn't. I knew coming here would let me think and decompress. It's still really raw."

"That was a smart move." Lydia nodded.

Angela realized she wasn't really ready to talk about the situation in detail yet. Her walk had cemented the fact that she didn't want to be married to Scott anymore, but she still didn't know any of the details of what she wanted to do with her life after. Thankfully, Lydia knew her well enough to not push for too many details, too fast.

"How are things with you?" Angela asked, shifting the conversation away from her recent troubles.

"Oh, you know." Lydia shrugged, glancing down at the sea-blue tablecloth. "About the same."

"Are you holding up well?" Angela didn't have to elaborate what she meant—they both knew she was talking about Paul's passing.

Angela only recently heard that Lydia had lost her husband a year ago through her parents, but she hadn't had Lydia's contact info to send flowers or reach out at the time of the funeral. Millie eventually passed along Lydia's address to Angela's parents, who passed it along to Angela. The flowers had been late, but Lydia had sent a thank you note anyway. Angela couldn't imagine going through that sort of grief.

"More or less." Lydia looked out the window for a moment. "It's still hard every day. I came back to Marigold just for a break, especially since work has been so busy."

"Because of the summer coming up?"

"Yep. Everyone's trying to get their trips planned."

The two women fell into lighter topics, chatting about how their careers were going and how their children were doing. They also reminisced about the fun times they'd had when they were their kids' ages. Even though it had been years since those days, it felt like hardly any time had passed at all. Between the easy flow of the conversation and the light warmth of the bisque, Angela found herself more relaxed than she'd been on a Saturday afternoon in a long time.

A while later, Lydia glanced out the window and did a subtle double take.

"Isn't that Patrick Devlin?" she asked, keeping her voice low as if he could hear them.

Angela followed Lydia's gaze outside and down the block a little way. Sure enough, it *was* Patrick. Angela couldn't forget his kind green eyes and his chestnut brown hair, even with his shadow of beard stubble and his slightly taller, more adult frame. He was even wearing a more grown-up version of the jeans and a dark t-shirt that he'd worn all the time back then.

Teenage Angela had devoted many pages in her diary to him, along with lots of hearts decorating the margins. Her mom probably still had that diary tucked away somewhere—not that Angela had any interest in digging it out. She was sure she couldn't re-read her old entries without cringing at least a little.

She'd told Lydia, Grace, and Rachel all about her crush on him during their summers together, sitting on the floor of Angela's bedroom on the nights they had sleepovers. Everything he'd done was significant to her back then, from the way he'd nodded hello to her when they bumped into each other at the grocery store to something as silly as him wearing his hair a little differently.

Of course, her friends hadn't considered the things Angela told them silly. Instead, they'd listened intently as Angela analyzed everything to death, their eager support helping her feel less alone in her feelings. Now as an adult, Angela realized how much they had helped her avoid some embarrassing situations with their advice.

Angela had used to casually ask her parents about how Patrick was after she left for college, up until Scott came into her life and distracted her from her high school crush. All she knew was that he'd married the girl he started dating senior year, Aubrey, and that they both had moved back to the island after they graduated from college.

Lydia waved and caught Patrick's eye as he walked by, making him break into an easy smile. He came inside the restaurant and strolled over to their table.

"Hey, ladies. Long time, no see," he said with a grin.

"Yeah, it's been a while!" Lydia smiled. "How have you been?"

Angela smiled too, nodding along at the appropriate times as Patrick and Lydia made polite small talk. For whatever reason, she suddenly felt like the tongue-tied teenager she'd once been around him. She couldn't even bring herself to rave about the delicious bisque they were finishing, even though it was the best thing she'd eaten in a long time.

Eventually, Patrick had to get back to his errands and left. Neither of the women said anything until the door to the restaurant had closed and Patrick had disappeared past the windows.

"Wow, he's certainly aged well," Lydia murmured, leaning forward a little and lowering her voice as if Patrick were still nearby. "He was pretty cute back then, but he looks even better all grown up."

Angela sipped her water and shrugged, hoping

her old friend wouldn't notice the slight flush in her cheeks.

"This was exactly what I needed," Lydia said as she and Angela walked on the beach later.

After lunch, they'd made their way to the beach to keep chatting. Both of them had taken off their shoes to feel the sand between their toes. Even though the day had become slightly overcast, the island still seemed to sparkle in Lydia's eyes. She'd forgotten how good being on Marigold felt. The slower pace, the smell of the sea, and the sounds of birds and boats soothed and energized her.

"Same here." Angela stepped around a cluster of seashells.

They alternated between chatting and walking in the comfortable silences that close friends can manage. Lydia hadn't seen Angela in years, but it felt like they had picked up right where they'd left off.

How long had it been since Lydia had felt like this with a friend? Way too long.

She definitely hadn't had a great time like this since Paul's death. In the two years between his diagnosis and his death, Lydia had spent most of her time with him or with Holly. Her friends back in Boston understood her, and she felt like she could lean on them for support, but somehow, the bonds she felt with Angela felt just as strong, even though they had lost touch for a while.

"Ah, the Beachside Inn!" Lydia said as they rounded a curve in the beach. "I hadn't realized we'd walked this far along the beach."

The Beachside Inn had been stunning in its prime, but even now in its run-down state, it had a certain stately allure to it. It was a massive two-story structure with white wood siding, bay windows that let in plenty of light no matter the time of day, and a huge porch where Lydia had spent many evenings with her friends and family growing up. Since Millie's home was small, Lydia and her parents had always stayed at the inn when they came to Marigold.

As they got closer, they saw the wear and tear on the outside. Some of the wood on the porch was starting to go, and it really needed a fresh coat of paint and a nice landscaping job. If the outside looked like that, the inside likely wasn't faring well either. The innkeeper's residence on the far side of the inn needed a new roof for sure, along with fresh paint. There was a *For Sale* sign on the edge of the property.

"Oh wow, I wonder how long it's been for sale," Angela said, gesturing toward the sign. "Things have been developing really quickly here, so I bet it hasn't been too long. My mom said they've been tearing down old buildings left and right to build updated ones."

Lydia frowned. The heart of her memories of Marigold were in this inn. All the delicious dinners, all the cozy, rainy evenings spent curled up with a book, all the laughter. She even remembered the smell—like the ocean mixed with that scent of home that was hard to put a specific name to.

"I hate that. I mean, I'm glad people are interested in Marigold, but the thought of bulldozing a historic place like this hurts my heart."

Lydia kicked at the sand. She and her friends had sat on this very beach having picnics and bonfires. If someone bought the Beachside Inn and tore it down, would future people be able to make memories just like hers in this very spot? Many of the new businesses Lydia had seen still blended well with Marigold's energy and spirit, but who knew how long that would last?

Angela stopped and stared at the building for a

second before looking back to Lydia. There was an undeniable spark in her bright blue eyes.

"What is it?" Lydia asked.

"This idea is pretty nuts, but hear me out," Angela said, looking back at the memory-filled inn. "What if... what if we bought the inn together and reopened it?"

CHAPTER FOUR

Lydia blinked, trying to absorb what Angela had said.

Buy the inn?

The idea felt so wild and daring that Lydia didn't know how to feel.

"Think about it—we both need a reset, and we both clearly miss this place a lot. It just feels good to be back on Marigold." Angela looked between her friend and the inn. "We can do both of those things if we buy the inn. It'll be both a fresh start and a reason to stay on the island, and we could fix it up in a way that honors what it used to be." She grinned, seeming to get more and more excited with each word. "I can use my design experience to make it gorgeous again, and your travel agent experience could help us shape it into a place that people are fighting to stay in."

Lydia nodded slowly, soaking in what her friend had said. It *was* a little hard to wrap her mind around what Angela was suggesting, but the thought of having a big project, something that she was truly passionate about in a place that made her feel alive again, was exciting. While she loved her job, it had been a while since any of the work she did felt fresh.

"It'll definitely need a lot of renovations on the inside since it's so old, but the bones are so good. And the location is stellar," Lydia said slowly, ideas starting to spin in her head. "I've had so many clients go to Marigold specifically for that New England coast experience, and this place would fit the bill perfectly."

Angela's smile was bigger than any Lydia had seen her wear all day.

"We could do it, though. I really think we could." Angela crossed her arms and assessed the inn again. She chewed on her lower lip, glancing at Lydia. "Is it a crazy idea?"

"A little crazy. I've done home renovations in the past, and they were a lot to deal with, but this feels different." Lydia shook her head, blowing out a breath. "We'd have to sit down and make a lot of plans."

"So, one of your favorite things?" Angela laughed. Even as kids, Lydia was the one who had organized all of their outings and sleepovers.

Lydia chuckled. "I do love a good plan. Why do you think I became a travel agent? It's planning and travel all rolled into one."

"We can add 'planning skills' to the 'pro' column, then," Angela said. The two women gazed up at the inn for several long moments before she added slowly, "I think we should do it."

"Really?"

"Yes. As scary as it is, as crazy as it is, I feel like it's exactly what I need."

Lydia nodded, her heart beating a little faster. "I think so too."

She tried to imagine what the inn could become with her and Angela's touch. They both had the skills to pull this off, even though it wasn't something either of them had ever done before. And they understood what made Marigold special and what the inn had been like in its prime, so they could preserve its spirit.

It was a wild idea, that was for sure.

But why not take the plunge?

* * *

"Guess who I ran into today?" Angela said to her mom later that evening as she pulled a sheet pan of brussels sprouts out of the oven. They were roasted to perfection, crispy and a little charred. "Lydia Walker."

"Really? How is she?" Phoebe placed a basket of rolls on the table next to the juicy pork tenderloin she'd made.

Brooke and Travis were there again, so Phoebe had gone all out for a second night in a row. Lured by the smell of food, Angela's siblings started to drift toward the dining room, and Mitch and Jake came in from out back to wash up before eating. Brooke poured herself and Travis a glass of Vinum Cellars Petite Sirah.

"She's doing fine." Angela put the sprouts in a big serving bowl, stuck a spoon in it, and took it to the table. "Actually, we had an idea that I want to bounce off all of you once we're all in here."

"What idea?" Brooke asked, putting her glass of wine down on the counter.

"A business idea. Come help with the mashed potatoes."

Brooke helped Angela while Travis sliced into

the rested pork tenderloin. Eventually, Mitch and Jake joined them, both of them all cleaned up from playing outside. Mitch looked as tired as you'd expect a man in his early sixties who'd just played all day with a six-year-old to be. Jake, for once, looked a little tired too. They had spent all day chasing after Mitch's friend's puppy and playing on the beach.

As everyone got their food and poured themselves some wine—or, in Jake's case, juice—Angela gathered her thoughts. She hadn't been able to stop thinking about the inn and everything she and Lydia could do to make it shine again, but she wanted some outside assurance. Her family always had her best interests at heart and were always honest without being harsh.

"So, about that business idea I mentioned," Angela said after a sip of wine. "Lydia and I are thinking of buying the old Beachside Inn, the one she and her family used to stay at every summer when we were growing up. We want to renovate it and bring it back to what it used to be. We hope a whole new generation of visitors can enjoy it the way Lydia did."

"Wow." Mitch sat back in his seat, his eyebrows lifting. "That's a big idea."

"It is." Angela let out a shaky sigh. "I could

decorate it, and I know a few people who could put me in touch with good contractors up here. It would need a lot of work—it looks a little rough from the outside, which probably means the floors and the pipes aren't looking so hot either. Lydia knows all sorts of hospitality industry people who could help us when we eventually open."

"Renovations are a pain. You're sure you can find the right contacts?" Travis asked, taking a bite of his mashed potatoes. "A place that old is bound to have some definite 'quirks' that will need to be fixed."

"I'm sure. Lydia's great at planning, and once she's got an itch, she won't stop until she sees things through." Angela smiled, thinking about how Lydia had already made a list of things to do by the time they'd gone their separate ways earlier.

Travis nodded, thinking about it. "It could work out, especially if you design it as well as you designed Mom and Dad's place."

Angela was proud of all the design she'd done for her parents' house. They trusted her enough to give her free rein and loved everything she had done. It was functional, practical, and cozy, which fit her parents to a tee.

"I already have a lot of ideas. I haven't been inside in a long time, but I remember there being a lot of great space for people to gather." Angela remembered eating dinner with Lydia's family at the inn a few times. "Maybe we could hold events there in the future. And there's a pretty large kitchen and dining area. I don't know what our entire budget will be, but I'm sure we could serve food eventually."

"Ooh, do you think I could bake for the inn?" Brooke asked. "I've gotten a lot of good feedback from friends—"

"—and from us," Mitch added, craning his neck to look longingly at the blondies Brooke had made, which were cooling in the kitchen. Brooke had gently smacked his hand away when he'd tried to snag one before dinner.

"Of course." Brooke's grin widened. "I think I'm ready to share my baking with strangers."

"That would be amazing!" Angela imagined people in a newly renovated sitting area, sipping tea and enjoying Brooke's desserts.

"All of that sounds fabulous, honey," Phoebe said. "We'll help out in any way we can. And doing this would mean that you and Jake would stay here, right?"

"Right." Angela glanced at her son, who was poking at a brussels sprout with his fork. "I think it would be good for both of us, considering everything that's going on in my life and Lydia's. I forgot how much I love being so close to you all too. We could do dinners like this every week."

Hearing that Angela wanted to stay made everyone perk up a little. Their conversations about Scott had been limited to the basics of what Angela was going to do, but either way, no one was a fan of Scott anymore. They definitely didn't want her to go back to a man who had cheated on her.

Angela looked down the table at Jake, who was curiously looking at all the adults around him.

"Jake, how do you feel about staying in Marigold? You'd get to make new friends at a new school and see everyone here more often." Angela held her breath, hoping her little boy would be happy with the idea. If he wasn't on board, she'd have to rethink everything.

"Hmm..." Jake absently kicked his legs, making him rock a bit. Then he nodded, beaming a broad grin. "Sounds cool!"

Angela let out the breath she'd been holding, taking in her son's excited face. He approved. Now everything—buying the inn, moving back to Marigold, starting over—all felt so much more real.

CHAPTER FIVE

After Lydia and Angela had parted ways, Lydia had sat down on a bench downtown and started adding to her list of things to do for the inn. Of course, they had to get their finances together and put an offer in on the building, but there were so many other things to do before that. By the time Lydia got back to Millie's for dinner, she was buzzing with excitement.

"Come sit and talk to me before you explode, Lyds," Millie said with a laugh, bringing two bowls of butternut squash risotto to her small dining room table. "What happened to you today?"

"Well, I ran into my old friend Angela in town. We ended up having lunch at that café you mentioned—the one with the great views." Lydia sat, putting a bottle of Pedroncelli wine and two glasses down. "The lobster bisque was incredible. I don't know what they put in it to make it that delicious, but I'll probably be dreaming of it tonight."

"Isn't it to die for? If there weren't a million other new restaurants on the island, I'd probably go there every week. Too much good food, not enough time." Millie popped the cork on the wine and poured them each a glass.

"We'll have to check out more of them together," Lydia said with a smile. "Anyway, the two of us caught up, and it was so wonderful. We've both had big shakeups in our lives recently, and it was so nice to reconnect. After lunch, we ended up walking down the beach. We stumbled on that inn where I used to stay with my parents every summer. The Beachside Inn. Apparently, it's for sale." She took a big breath, a giddy feeling passing through her as she spoke the words out loud. "We want to buy it, fix it up, and reopen it." She grinned. "It's going to be a lot of work, but I think we can do it. I've already started making to-do lists and sketching out what we want the inn to be."

"Well, that is just about the best idea I've heard all year. I miss that place," Millie said, raising her wine glass. "We have to toast to it. And to you staying in Marigold, I'm guessing?"

"Yep!" Lydia clinked her glass against Millie's. "I don't think we could do this if I was back in Boston and Angela was in Philly. We'll both move here."

Millie's smile broadened even more, and happiness warmed Lydia's chest. Finally, they could spend more time together. Lydia missed staying up late, talking to Millie about anything under the sun. Her aunt had lived on Marigold for a long time, but that didn't mean she lacked life experience. She had stories that kept Lydia amused and smiling for hours after.

"It's a good thing you two stumbled upon the inn," Millie said. "It's been closed for a while, and I was afraid we'd lose it."

"What happened to it?"

"The older couple that ran it—the Stewarts—died, and their son didn't do much with it." Millie shrugged. "He lives off the island too."

Lydia raised an eyebrow and swallowed a bite of her risotto. "He didn't want to keep it up and running? Why not? It's such a beautiful place."

"The Stewarts were having trouble keeping the inn busy, especially in this day and age. There's so much competition out here now." Millie shook her head and sipped her wine. "But don't worry—it wasn't a matter of tourists not wanting to come to

Marigold. The Stewarts just didn't have the energy to do all the marketing, and the lack of business made it hard for them to maintain the place."

Lydia's confidence in the project slipped a bit. Sure, renovations took a lot of energy, but what if the Stewarts didn't do them because they knew it was going to be a money pit? She tried to remember the details of the inn, at least the ones she could see. Was the roof on the inn in okay shape? How was the insulation in the innkeeper's house? Since it hadn't been occupied, was there water damage that she couldn't see?

The two women finished up their risotto and wine, catching each other up on the events of the day.

"I think I'm going to take a peek at the inn again this evening," Lydia said as she rinsed her risotto dish. "Just to double check a few things before I get too excited about this idea."

"Okay, sounds good." Millie patted Lydia on the shoulder. "But I really do think it's a great plan."

"Thanks. I'll bring back something from The Sweet Creamery," Lydia added. She was still thinking about that red velvet cake ice cream they'd had the night before.

"Did you know you're my absolute favorite

person right now?" Millie laughed. "Surprise me with the flavor!"

Lydia hopped in her car and drove the short distance to the inn. She parked her car in the slightly overgrown lot next to the building and got out, turning toward the sun as it set over the water. Even though she'd seen them time and time again throughout her life, the sunsets on Marigold still enthralled her. The sky was a brilliant blend of orange, pink, and purple, speckled with the shadows of boats on the water out toward the horizon.

She sat on a big rock to watch the sun go all the way down. She had sat on this very rock with Angela and her other friends, or with her parents and Millie. It was the best spot to take in the view, so they'd scrambled to get there early when they wanted to watch the sunset. Her mother would bring snacks like trail mix with chocolate or popcorn for them to munch on as they talked, waiting for the main event. She and her dad would sometimes play cards, finding smooth spots on the rock to lay their cards down.

After the sun dipped below the horizon, Lydia looked back at the inn. She couldn't let this place go. Now that she was back on Marigold, back at the Beachside Inn, she realized how significant it had been in her life. She could give other families the same incredible memories she'd had. Just because the project might be difficult didn't mean it wasn't worth pursuing.

Lydia pulled out her phone and called Holly to tell her daughter their plans for the inn. As always, there was some noise in the background when Holly picked up. People were talking loudly and laughing on top of some upbeat electronic music.

"Hey, Mom! Sorry, sorry. People are playing some video game in the common room," Holly said, the sound going quiet as she slipped into her room and shut her bedroom door. "What's up? How are you?"

"I'm great. I actually wanted to tell you something," Lydia said.

She gave Holly the full run-down of Angela's and her plans for the inn, surprised at how lively she sounded as she spoke. She hadn't even realized how low-energy she'd been lately, even when she got a good night's rest. Her sluggishness had run deeper than lack of sleep.

"Mom, that sounds amazing!" Lydia could easily imagine Holly bouncing up from her spot on her bed. "It sounds like the perfect thing for you. And you get to do it with a friend."

"Yeah, I've missed Angela. It feels like we've

picked up like we were never apart." Lydia kicked off her shoes and wandered toward the water a little. It was much cooler at night, but she preferred to be a little cold than to have sand in her sneakers.

"That's so great. I'm really happy for you." Something shuffled on Holly's side of the line and she paused. "Um, Aiden's asking if I want to go with everyone for pad Thai, and I'm starving. I'll talk to you later, okay?"

"Aiden? Who is Aiden?"

The moment the words were out of her mouth, Lydia realized that she sounded exactly like her mother always had when Lydia had mentioned a boy as a teenager. She didn't mind that she was turning into her mother since she'd loved her mom dearly, but wow, did she feel old.

"Just... he's a friend. I really gotta go. Love you, bye."

Holly hung up, and Lydia laughed. She'd have to get more information about this Aiden the next time they talked. He had to be someone special, just based on the way Holly had rushed her off the phone. Lydia tucked her phone back into her bag and walked closer to the water. It was still freezing cold, so she stopped before the waves washed over her toes.

She hadn't told a soul about it, but sometimes she talked to Paul when she was alone. Even though she couldn't see him or touch him, she felt like talking out loud would somehow bring him closer to her. At the very least, she felt less empty.

"I'm really doing this, aren't I?" Lydia asked, looking out onto the water. "I think is the thing that you told me to do, Paul. It's pretty crazy when I think about it, and I'm just as excited as I am scared. I'll have Angela, and it's so lovely to be back in each other's lives, but I really wish you were here to see me through this."

A tear slipped down her cheek and she wiped it away, only for another to replace it. She dabbed at her eyes, then jumped like a startled cat when she heard footsteps on the seashells behind her.

She whirled around and saw a man walking along the shore, just close enough to have heard her talking to herself. He must have been taking a stroll just like she was, his hands tucked into the pockets of his light, comfortable-looking jacket and a baseball cap on his head.

Mortified, Lydia tucked her wind-blown hair behind her ears and made her way back up to her car quickly. She hoped the man hadn't heard her. A total stranger didn't need to know about her somewhat unusual method of coping with her grief.

She started her car and pulled away, trying not to look back at where the man was standing on the beach.

Grant Hamlin watched the woman quickly walk off the beach, her arms crossed.

Even with her face tilted down and the evening setting in, he could see the pink flush of her cheeks. He briefly wondered if he should say something—not that he knew what he'd say. She had clearly been in the middle of a private moment when he'd walked past, and he hadn't intended to intrude.

He kept walking, tucking his hands into his pockets again. Why had she caught his eye? She hadn't been the only person he'd passed on the beach as he walked, although it wasn't that busy. Maybe he was drawn to how vulnerable she'd looked, her brown hair stirred by the wind. She'd looked like she was deep in a difficult thought, like she was struggling with something.

He knew the feeling well. He'd come out on this walk to get away from the quiet inside his home, which was still overwhelming two years after losing his wife, Annie. The house wasn't big since it had been just the two of them, and he hadn't gotten rid of any of her things, but it felt like it had doubled in size since her passing.

"Letting go is really hard, Annie," Grant said quietly.

He'd gotten used to talking to her like this, staring out onto the water. It was one of the few ways he could cope when the loneliness got too intense. The sounds of the waves and the crunch of the sand beneath his shoes calmed him, even though they also reminded him of Annie in many ways. The two of them had walked on this beach together countless times, holding hands and talking about their days. It was almost as if a little piece of her lived here, along with his other memories of the ocean and sand. The fresh air could always calm him down, even as a child.

He blew out a heavy sigh and watched a boat drift toward the dock as the sun sank below the horizon.

"I know you told me you wanted me to let go when it was time, but I still don't know how to do that. Every time I look at our bedroom or that couch we bought on a whim, I think about you." He went quiet for a moment as he passed by a couple chatting. When they were out of earshot, he continued, speaking low under his breath. "But I need to *make* it the right time. I've got to let go, even if it hurts. But I won't forget you, ever. I love you so much."

Grant took another deep breath and let it out, letting the salty air clear his head.

He had to let go.

He was tired of living in the past, thinking of the spaces where Annie should have been at every turn. It was holding him back from really living, from being the man he remembered being when Annie was alive.

Now was a good a time as ever to take the plunge.

CHAPTER SIX

Angela stared at her phone in her hand, Scott's cell number already punched in. Unlike many of the numbers in her phone, she'd had his memorized for years. All she had to do was dial him up. She took a deep breath and called him. It was Monday morning, and she knew that he was working from home—or at least, he *should* be. Sure enough, he answered on the second ring.

"Angie?" He spoke quickly. "How are you?"

"I'm fine. Jake is too." Angela swallowed. "How are you?"

"I'm okay. I'm just working on emails for a while before I head into the office for a meeting."

There was a long, uncomfortable pause. They were dancing around the issue, as Angela had expected. Everything had shifted so quickly that she wasn't sure how to go about doing something as simple as making small talk with the man she had been with for over a decade.

She had spent most of the rest of her weekend figuring out how to say this. She had never thought she would have to speak the words she was about to say, but she would have to find the strength to do it now. There was a knot in her chest that kept pulling tighter and tighter the longer she waited to speak.

"Scott, I want a divorce," she said in one breath. Right to the point, just as she'd practiced. The knot in her chest was still tight, but at least it wasn't getting any tighter. "I don't know if I can go forward with our marriage knowing you weren't faithful."

Scott let out a long breath on his side of the line. Angela could easily see him tugging at his hair the way he did when he was frustrated. Most of the time, she saw him do it while he was watching sports or working.

"I can't tell you how sorry I am, Angela. I really can't." This time, Angela could tell he was being entirely truthful. "If you want a divorce, I'll do it. But if you give me another chance, I'll do better. I promise. I don't want to lose you."

Angela picked at a loose thread on the bedspread

in her parents' guest room. She didn't doubt that Scott would try. But who was to say he'd keep his word, considering he'd strayed before? Walking in on him once had been bad enough, but the thought of going through it *again* after him saying he wouldn't was too painful to imagine.

"I don't think so, Scott. I just don't think I can do it. I want a divorce." Angela gently squeezed her knee. "I'll get started on it and get in touch, okay?"

"Okay." He let out a deep breath. There was a long pause, and Angela wondered if Scott would argue or try harder to convince her. But instead, all he said was, "Talk soon."

"Bye."

Angela lay back onto her bed after she hung up the phone and pressed the heels of her hands to her eyes. The call had lasted less than five minutes—what else could they have said, anyway?—but she felt like a small piece of the burden on her shoulders had been lifted.

Now the ball was in her court, something she was far more comfortable with. On top of the work she had on the inn and emails from her job, she had to research divorce lawyers and start that process. It was a lot, but it had to be done.

After she decompressed from the call, she

finished getting dressed and headed out to meet with Lydia at Titan Real Estate Partners, a few blocks off Main Street. It was in a small white building connected to a pharmacy, its bright blue wooden sign hanging out front. The front window was filled with pictures of listings, both commercial and residential, along with the contact information for all the real estate agents. It seemed like the market in Marigold was doing well for itself, even though it was a small place.

Angela pushed the door open, making the bell jingle. This time, the flutter in her stomach was from the good kind of nerves. Never one to waste any time, Lydia had set up their appointment with a real estate agent to talk about buying the inn.

Lydia had gotten there first and was waiting in the lobby. She was dressed semi-casually in jeans, ankle boots, and a cowl neck sweater in a light green that brought out the color of her eyes. The two women hugged and sat down, fidgeting excitedly and sticking to small talk. Not long after Angela arrived, their real estate agent, Jennifer Lowry, came out to greet them.

"Lydia and Angela?" Jennifer asked, popping her head around the corner. She was probably a few years younger than both of them, with a warm, pretty smile. Angela had noticed her picture next to several of the listings in the front window.

"That's us," Angela said, standing.

"Awesome, come on back."

They made their way into Jennifer's office and took a seat. The space was small, but Angela noticed how well laid out it was to maximize its square footage. Jennifer had an air of competence about her that put Angela at ease, despite the significance of what they were about to discuss.

"So, you two are interested in the Beachside Inn." Jennifer clicked around on her computer a bit, presumably pulling up information about the inn.

"We are." Lydia folded her hands in her lap. "I used to stay there all the time during the summer growing up, so when we saw it was for sale, we had to jump on the chance."

"That's so lovely. It really is a beautiful space." Jennifer looked away from her computer screen for a moment, shooting them a smile. "And luckily, the buying process should be pretty simple. There haven't been any other offers on the house, and the seller is very motivated."

Angela let out a breath she hadn't even realized she'd been holding. "That's great to hear. I'm a little surprised, honestly."

Jennifer lifted a shoulder. "I am too. It's such a classic New England style inn, and more and more businesses have been cropping up. It's the perfect investment with the bump of tourism we've been experiencing. But I do see how it would be intimidating. It is pretty old, and some people get scared off by big projects like this."

"Yeah, we're a little afraid of that too," Lydia said. "But it's worth the risk. I don't want it to get torn down or turned into something generic. Do you have information on what updates it would need to come up to code?"

"Not a complete list yet—we'd have to get the inspector in to get accurate details. But I can tell you that there's work to be done."

Angela and Lydia nodded. They were ready for it, though Angela was still worried about what they'd find. Travis was right to question how worthwhile it would be to update everything, even though he was ultimately supportive of the idea.

"We're up for the challenge. I'm an interior designer and Lydia works in the travel industry, so this should be something we can put our current skill sets to." Angela smiled.

"This does sound perfect! There are a lot of great inns here, but nothing in that particular area. Getting this place up and running will be great for the island." Jennifer glanced between the two women. "Also, if you'd like to take a closer look inside, we're having an open house on Saturday. But since you're here, you can put in your offer before that. Would you like to do that?"

Angela and Lydia looked at each other, both excited.

"Let's do it!" Angela said.

Jennifer walked them through the process of putting in their offer, then escorted them out, shaking both of their hands before they parted ways. To celebrate, Lydia and Angela took a stroll down near the water to a seafood restaurant that neither of them had tried before. They split an indulgent lobster mac n' cheese topped with toasted breadcrumbs and a lighter, but no less delicious, spring greens salad with salmon, jotting down their next steps.

"I'm so excited," Lydia said, looking down at the list she'd made on a notepad from her purse. The whole page was filled with ideas. "It's starting to feel real. This is happening."

"Cheers to the future." Angela lifted her glass of iced tea.

"To the future," Lydia echoed, tapping her tea against Angela's.

They finished up their meal and headed back toward their cars, which they'd left in the parking lot of the real estate office. As they approached the lot, Angela's phone started to ring.

"Oh, it's Jennifer!" Angela scrambled to answer it. "Hello?"

"Hi, Angela, it's Jennifer Lowry, from Titan. I know we just finished our meeting not long ago, but I just wanted to give you an update." The tone of the real estate agent's voice made Angela's stomach twist. "There's been another offer on the house, so this might not be as simple as we thought."

* * *

Lydia had been on pins and needles all week. The inn hadn't left her mind for more than an hour or so the whole time.

With the other offer on the inn, it felt like the buyer wanted to push them into a bidding war. She and Angela had gone over their finances, and they had just enough money to buy the inn and do the expected renovations before opening it to guests—and not much more. Both of them were dipping well into their savings already. She didn't know what she'd do if they lost a bidding war.

Lydia ran a hand through her brunette hair as she pulled around the corner and drove into the lot next to the Beachside Inn. The parking lot was filled with cars today, including Angela's. They had all come for the open house, and that made Lydia even more uneasy.

What if someone else put in an offer? There was no way they'd keep up with a third person in the mix.

"Hey," Lydia said to Angela, who was standing out front. "You ready?"

"Ready as I'll ever be." Her friend managed to smile, but Lydia could tell she was nervous too. "There are more people here than I thought there would be."

"Same here."

They walked through the inn's open front door, and instantly, Lydia was awash with memories. The place had aged, certainly, but it was still just as beautiful in its own way as it had always been.

The bones of the house were better than anything they could create through renovations—the high ceilings, natural light, and sturdy build were almost priceless. The dated wallpaper was starting to come down in some corners, someone had put in some unattractive carpet in some areas, and the wood floors that were left were badly in need of refinishing, but the way the realtor had staged the home pushed those minor flaws aside.

Someone had opened the bay windows all over the inn, letting in the fresh ocean air, and all the furniture had a fresh polish on it. With a tiny bit of updating and elbow grease, it could be spectacular.

People were standing around, chatting and nibbling on the finger foods that had been laid out next to pamphlets with information about the inn. Lydia snagged a small plate and loaded it with salmon blini and little cucumber sandwiches while Angela did the same.

They wandered around the space together, Angela eyeing the other potential buyers and Lydia sliding into her memories. The common space where she'd played cards with her dad was still laid out in the same way. She remembered wanting to slide down the heavy wood railing into the lobby, although she'd never gotten the chance to do it.

After a little while, Angela split off to go look at the dining area while Lydia went farther into the inn to one of her favorite old reading spots, another bay window. She stood and looked out onto the water. It was a chilly day, but she wouldn't have known it from the bright sunshine streaming through the window. Lydia hoped she could experience this view during the summer again.

"You must really like the water, huh?" a man said from behind her.

Lydia jumped, nearly sending the remains of her finger food onto the bay window seat. She turned to see who had spoken, and to her surprise, it was the man who had caught her talking to herself on the beach the other evening. Now that she wasn't so wildly embarrassed, she could actually meet his gaze and get a good look at him.

He was probably around her age, in his very late thirties or early forties, and had the rugged exterior of a man who wasn't a stranger to working outside. His brown eyes were serious, which seemed to be his default expression—the few lines on his skin were more like frown lines instead of crow's feet from smiling all the time. All in all, he was handsome in the way that Lydia liked; he didn't seem too conscious of his good looks.

"I'm sorry, what did you say?" she said, flushing a little as she realized she was staring blankly at him.

"The water. It's a nice view." Gesturing to the bay window, he came to stand next to her. He tucked his hands into the pockets of his jeans. "I like this section of the beach."

"I do too." Lydia smiled softly. "I came to this inn every summer when I was a girl, and I used to curl up on this seat and read whenever the weather was too bad to go outside."

The man just nodded. He seemed to be totally fine with silence.

"I'm Lydia Walker, by the way." She extended her hand.

"Grant Hamlin." He turned slightly to face her, tugging one hand out of his pocket to shake hers. His palm was roughened slightly by callouses, confirming her suspicion that he worked with his hands at least some of the time. "Are you looking to put in an offer on the place?"

"I already have. My friend and I have, I mean." Lydia smiled. "I'm a travel agent and she's an interior designer, so we want to refurbish the place and reopen it."

"Ah." He didn't seem impressed, lifting one eyebrow in an almost challenging expression. "You don't think it would be better to just tear the whole place down and start over? Makes more sense."

"What? Of course not," Lydia said. "Can't you see how beautiful the bones of this place are? It's a piece of history. I can't imagine letting this kind of landmark get turned into a boring old place you could find anywhere."

"But with those beautiful old bones comes expensive upkeep. The pipes are probably shot, the foundation is most likely a wreck, and there's probably rotted wood everywhere." Grant glanced around the frame of the window and tapped a spot where the paint was chipped and the wood was a little split. "Spots like this. If I'm the winning bidder, I'll probably tear it down and start over."

"Wait. *You're* the other bidder?"

Lydia's heart started pounding, and she crossed her arms over her chest. She didn't want to lose the inn, of course, but if the other bidder won, refurbished, and re-opened it, she wouldn't be completely devastated. She couldn't bear the idea of losing the bidding war *and* the inn though.

"I am." He swept some paint chips off his fingertips. "The land has great potential for something a little more practical—maybe a commercial space since so many restaurants and shops have been opening up lately."

Lydia's mouth gaped open. Grant wasn't kidding. He would really do it. How could he walk around this gorgeous place and only see the things that needed work? There were so many beautiful things about the inn.

"You seriously think that would be better for Marigold? People come here for history, too, you know." Lydia was surprised at her tone. She never sassed strangers like this.

"How much is that history worth to you, Lydia?" One of his eyebrows went up, and the ghost of what might have been a smile came into his eyes. Lydia couldn't tell.

"A whole lot, actually."

Looking up at his square, stubbled jaw took a bit of the wind out of her sails. It had been a while since she'd found a man to be this attractive. Too bad he was the one person who could crush her dreams.

Grant shrugged, holding her gaze. "Well, the thought of something new is worth a lot to me."

"We'll just have to see whose offer gets accepted, then."

"I guess we will."

They stared at each other for a few heartbeats, and Lydia had to make a conscious effort not to scowl at him.

Who did this guy think he was? He talked about his plans in such a passive way, like he just wanted to get them over with to make a few bucks. He didn't seem like the kind of guy with a lot of joy in his life. But why did he have to try to ruin *her* joy?

Angela interrupted their stare-off moments later.

"Oh, there you are, Lydia!" she said, stepping off the staircase. "Come upstairs with me. I want to show you one of the guest rooms and bounce some ideas off of you."

"Okay." Lydia nodded at the man with the serious face and deep brown eyes. "Nice to meet you, Grant."

"Likewise," he said, dipping his chin.

But *had* it been nice to meet him?

Her face heated up as she followed Angela up the stairs to the second floor. Grant Hamlin was the embodiment of the worst outcome for the inn, but maybe she shouldn't have gotten on his case like that. He had just as much of a right to put an offer in on the inn as she did.

Something about Grant threw Lydia off balance, but she couldn't focus on that now. She had an inn to buy.

CHAPTER SEVEN

Lydia hadn't been to Angela's family's home in decades, but it still had the same warm, inviting exterior that she remembered, from the chimneyed roof right down to the bushes Phoebe had planted beneath each of the front windows. The front door was cracked open, letting the sounds of Angela's family spill out into the yard.

The moment Lydia and Millie walked in, they were overwhelmed with greetings from everyone.

It was a full house—both Phoebe and Mitch were there, plus Angela, Jake, and Angela's siblings. It had been ages since Lydia had seen Travis and Brooke, and she could hardly believe how different and grown up they looked. The last time she had seen them, Travis was a gangly fourteen-year-old and Brooke was in middle school.

Millie had run into Phoebe and Mitch in town earlier in the week, so they picked right back up with a chat about wine that they'd had a few weeks ago. Even though Lydia had seen her aunt interact with people time and time again, she was still astonished by how personable and enthusiastic Millie was with everyone she knew.

Jake was just as energetic and sweet as Angela had said he was, only taking a moment to say hi before running off into the house. Lydia couldn't help but smile. She remembered Holly being that age and having that same seemingly endless energy.

Between Jake's excitement and the happy air of the gathering, the house was bursting with positive energy. Lydia hoped the celebratory atmosphere would be warranted.

They were still in limbo, waiting anxiously to see if their offer would be accepted. It could easily be rejected, if Grant or anyone else from the open house put in an offer that was more appealing. If that happened, she would have to go back to Philadelphia and figure out what to do next. She didn't want to think about all the awkward conversations she'd have to have if their plans fell through. She had already told so many people about what she and Angela wanted to do, and she didn't want to disappoint them.

But mostly, she didn't want to disappoint herself. As scary as it was to take the leap into co-owning a business, she'd gotten her heart set on reopening the inn.

It took a few moments, but eventually they all headed into the dining room and settled around the table. With Millie and Lydia there, everyone was almost elbow to elbow, but no one cared. There was too much good food laid out for anyone to worry about being cramped. Millie poured the Montinore Estate Pinot Noir she'd brought, and everyone grabbed food from the generously filled bowls that Phoebe had placed in the middle of the table.

Tonight Phoebe had made a delicious lamb Bolognese to go over some fresh pasta that Mitch and Jake—but mostly Mitch—had made together. It went perfectly with the wine, filling Lydia's belly with a warm coziness that was perfect for a nippy night. She hadn't eaten this many great meals in a row in years.

As they ate, everyone talked a little about their days. Since Phoebe and Mitch were retired, they'd had all day to play with Jake. They clearly adored him, and he adored them too. Millie had planted some new herbs in her garden, and Travis filled them in on what was happening in his job as a police officer. Marigold was very safe, so most of his day had been filled with mundane calls and interactions with his fellow officers. He had been a cop for years, which surprised Lydia. She never would've guessed the boy she once knew would decide to become a police officer.

"I still can't believe you two are adults, honestly." She chuckled, glancing at where Travis and Brooke were sitting across the table. "The last time I saw you, you were barely teenagers."

"Time flies," Travis said with a smile.

"It really does." Brooke shook her head, her blue eyes going wide. "Some of the kids I tutor are probably around the same age I was when we last saw each other. They feel so young sometimes."

"Oh, you're a tutor now? That's great!" Lydia said. "How do you like it? What subjects do you work with?"

"English and social studies, mostly. I love the kids, but I'm not sure if it's for me in the long run."

"Do you want to follow in your mom's footsteps?" Lydia asked. Phoebe had been an elementary school teacher before retiring.

"I don't think so. I've been teaching myself how to bake, so I think I want to open my own bakery someday." Brooke's cheeks flushed, as if she was unsure of herself.

"I'm sure you will. I can tell those brownies you made for dessert are going to be delicious, just from the smell." Millie gave Brooke a reassuring smile. She took a sip of her wine, then gave a little sigh. "And those little cookies filled with raspberry jam were a hit at the City Council meeting."

"Those were amazing. And the police department will be first in line when you open your bakery," Travis agreed. "Everyone at the station can't stop raving about every single treat of yours that they've tried. Sometimes they get antsy when they go a few days without something new."

Brooke laughed. "Good to know all of those cookies are being appreciated. My freezer is stuffed with all the things I'm able to freeze even though I'm the only one using it. I should give you more."

"Oh, I appreciate them, but I'm a single guy. I can't eat an entire batch of cookies on my own three times a week unless I grow an extra stomach." He twirled his fork in his pasta. "Trust me, I've tried."

Everyone laughed. Before anyone could say anything else, Angela's phone rang. The entire table went quiet. Usually, no one would answer their phone at a family dinner, but when she held the phone up, Lydia could see that the caller ID said it was Jennifer. The warm, content feeling she had in her belly from the food quickly changed into a ball of tight anxiety.

Angela answered, pushing her chair back a little to stand up before stepping into the next room. Not that it mattered, since everyone was watching her in anticipation through the open French doors.

"Uh-huh... yes, of course..." Angela caught Lydia's eye, breaking into a big smile. "Yes, that sounds perfect. Okay, bye."

"Well?" Mitch asked.

"We got the inn! The seller took our offer!" Angela declared, beaming.

Everyone cheered, raising their glasses. A massive weight lifted off Lydia's shoulders and was replaced with a blissful energy and a buzz of excitement.

This was it. The first step toward a new future.

"Whew, who knew I had this much stuff?" Angela asked, dropping one of the final boxes into what would become her bedroom in the innkeeper's residence. Her bed frame was set up, but her mattress was still wrapped in its protective plastic.

"It never looks like much until you have to pack it all into boxes," Lydia said, putting down a box beside her.

That was true. The moving truck filled with all of Angela and Jake's belongings had been packed to the brim when they'd left Philadelphia. She had taken nearly all the decorative pieces since Scott said he only needed the basics. The throw pillows, big mirrors, wall art, and knick-knacks that Angela had carefully and lovingly purchased over the years felt like half the load.

Packing up all of their things, putting in her notice at her old job, and dealing with the beginning of Scott's and her divorce all in a short few weeks had left Angela exhausted.

Especially the divorce. Scott had gone along with the preliminary steps, discussing their plans for Jake and how to split their assets, but he kept promising that his infidelity was a mistake he'd never make again. Still, Angela wasn't entirely convinced, despite his constant efforts. She had trusted Scott in the past, but now everything he did seemed to have a question mark hanging over it. She questioned his motives and his truthfulness at every turn.

She looked out the window to where Jake was running around with Brooke, who had come over to help keep the little boy out of the way of the movers. Both of them were laughing, putting Angela at ease. She'd made the right choice. Jake would have so much more space to run around here. Plus, they were so much closer to family.

Angela and Lydia headed back downstairs. Everywhere Angela looked, she saw potential. The wallpaper definitely needed to go—a fresh coat of light paint would make the space so much more bright and open. And the carpet on the stairs, which had been added somewhat recently, would go too. The wood beneath would be gorgeous with a little help. The rooms themselves would need the most time and attention from a design standpoint. She loved that each room had its own style and didn't want to change that.

They stopped in the entryway. It was a grand space, with high ceilings and natural light pouring in from the windows, but the light fixtures and rug were only making it seem smaller and closed in. A new chandelier was a must, as was a new rug. She knew just the right place to find them.

"I've worked up an appetite. Want to eat lunch in the innkeeper's residence?" Lydia asked.

"Definitely."

They went out to the innkeeper's residence, gathering Jake and saying goodbye to Brooke, who had to head out for an early afternoon tutoring session. They put together grilled cheese sandwiches using some local cheese Angela had found at the grocery store and a bit of leftover soup that Millie had given them since they were too busy to cook.

"Should we make this a working lunch?" Lydia cocked an eyebrow as she settled in at the table.

"That sounds like a plan." Angela looked around until she found a pen and pad of paper, then headed back to the dining table. "I can't wait to get started."

"Me neither, even though I'm super tired. There's so much to do." Lydia took a bite of her sandwich. "Where do you want to start?"

"Well, my selfish impulse is to start with the design part." Angela smiled. "But we can't design something before we fix it."

"That's true." Lydia grabbed her laptop and opened it. "We've got this list of things from the inspector to fix. I can manage the repairs side of things and you can take design, if that works for you."

"Sounds perfect."

Lydia made a spreadsheet of potential costs and their budget. Once they got through the repairs and estimated how much they could spend on each one, they shifted to the design. Angela's heart fluttered when she saw the amount of money she likely had to work with.

"Okay, I can work with this amount, I think," she said, scrolling up the spreadsheet and nodding. "I feel like I've been equally scared and excited ever since this started. I've never been able to have this much control over a project, besides my own home."

"It's going to look amazing. You care about this place just as much as I do, and I trust you to do it justice." Lydia opened a new tab in the spreadsheet.

"I hope so." Angela felt a tiny amount of self-doubt. She'd always done well within the boundaries that clients set, and she could do whatever she wanted in her own home, but how would she do with the future of the inn in mind? She hoped she wouldn't overthink everything.

"What are you thinking overall?" Lydia asked.

"I want to make it look updated without looking trendy or too modern for the space. I think it could look so much brighter, too. All the wallpaper has to go, or has to be replaced with something from this century. Same with the bathroom tiles." Angela tapped her pen on her paper. "I want to do something different in each room, just like it is now. It makes this place special."

"What about the common spaces?"

"I definitely want to keep the furniture, at least the stuff that can be spruced up. And we can save money, since I know how to do a lot of that myself."

Angela thought back to some work she'd done on an old dresser. It had turned out beautifully. All the furniture the inn had now could be just as beautiful if they gave it a bit of love. Each piece was crafted with the kind of care that had grown increasingly uncommon.

"Oh, yeah. That sounds amazing. With some elbow grease, the furniture will be gorgeous." Lydia typed up a few notes.

"I think I want to take a look at what the town has to offer. It would be great to support local businesses and artists." Angela jotted down some more notes, feeling confident again. She had this under control. It would turn out well if she trusted herself.

"I love that." Lydia nodded. "There's an art gallery in town, and I know there's a street fair once a month when the weather gets warmer. We can definitely find something there."

"I can't wait to see what we manage to put together."

Angela wrote down a list of design elements that had to be taken care of, from the bigger things like bathroom tiles and bathtubs, to the smaller things like art. She glanced at Jake, who was hard at work at his coloring pages. "Do you want to go shopping with me, Jake? We can look at paint colors and other fun stuff."

"Yeah!" He nodded enthusiastically, looking up at her.

"Let's finish up lunch and we can go, okay?" Angela pushed the rest of his sandwich toward him.

They finished the rest of their lunches, then Angela and Jake headed out to the car to drive into town. She couldn't wait to start, even though she knew the renovations and decorations would be the biggest project she'd ever undertaken.

CHAPTER EIGHT

Patrick Devlin stared at his computer screen but didn't really see any of the words he'd written. Not that there were many of them at all.

He sighed heavily and rubbed his tired eyes, turning his attention to the ocean and beachfront that were visible outside the window of his writing nook.

Writing had been a total slog lately. On a good day, the words just flowed out, and even if it was a terrible early draft, he felt proud of getting it done. But now, nothing felt right. His body was in his comfortable leather chair, but his mind was somewhere else.

He got up to get the blood flowing to his legs, wandering out of his office and into the hallway. The house was even quieter than usual since he had separated from his wife, Aubrey, and he still wasn't used to the silence. Both of them were fairly quiet, but he hadn't realized how many small sounds she made, from laughing at whatever she was reading in the living room to making a cup of tea.

Their separation had hit him hard. After several months of marriage counseling, she had sat him down one day a few weeks ago, her pretty features more serious than he'd seen them in a long time. It had scared the life out of him—he'd wondered if she was seriously ill or if she'd lost her job. The thought of her wanting to take time apart hadn't even crossed his mind as one of the possibilities, but that was exactly what she had wanted to discuss.

Despite the fact that he couldn't stop thinking about their relationship, he didn't know how to fix their marriage. Counseling had helped a little, but it had also revealed issues that he didn't know how to overcome.

Aubrey was visiting her family in Connecticut so that both of them could take the time apart to think, but his thoughts kept going around in unproductive circles. He had thought everything was fine before she first revealed she was unhappy in their relationship. They went out on semi-regular dates, got along well enough, and didn't really fight much.

But still, when she'd brought up the idea of counseling, she'd admitted that she hadn't been happy for a long time. In her words, she felt like she was going through the motions.

So, clearly, things weren't as fine as he had thought.

He wracked his brain for signs that she'd been unsatisfied and couldn't come up with any clear-cut examples. Some days, she was low on energy and wanted some time alone, but she had always been like that for as long as he'd known her. She went out more often with her friends than he did, but that was fine with him—he was a bit of a homebody sometimes and knew that she liked to have a girls' night out every once in a while. They'd had a few arguments over silly things like who was going to wash the trash cans or empty the dishwasher, but they always made up afterward.

That thought put him at the beginning of the circle his brain had been stuck on again.

They had been together since high school. How could he not have seen that the woman he knew better than anyone wasn't happy? How had he missed the fact that she wanted her life to go in a completely different direction than the one he'd thought they both wanted?

He ran his hands through his chestnut brown hair and stood, stretching his arms into the air. He needed to get out of the house, to be around people.

Their home was a ten-minute walk from town, which had been a big selling point when he and Aubrey had bought the house. Aubrey always wanted to go out and try all the new restaurants and bars, so the distance from the heart of it all was one of her favorite things. In moments like this, Patrick was glad they were close to town too. Once he got onto Main Street, he knew exactly what would help break his writer's block.

He went into The Sweet Creamery and ordered a waffle cone filled with three scoops—dark chocolate, cherry, and vanilla bean. Sometimes he liked to go with their more exotic flavors, but he was craving the classics today. He paid and tucked his wallet back into his pocket.

The moment the door shut behind him, something bumped into his legs. His grip on his ice cream cone wasn't enough to stop it from flying onto the ground.

"Oh no, I'm so, so sorry." Angela Collins came running up behind the child that had run into him.

He was clearly her son—the little guy took after her with his big blue eyes.

Before he ran into her and Lydia when he was running errands the other day, Patrick hadn't seen Angela since high school. But he remembered her. He'd worked on the literary magazine, and sometimes they would do projects with the art club, which she had been a part of. She'd seemed a little shy, but she'd opened up after the two clubs worked together for a while.

"Jake, honey, you need to watch where you're going," Angela added, resting her hands on her son's shoulder. "What do you say when you do something like this?"

"I'm sorry," the little boy said, looking genuinely guilty.

"It's okay, buddy." Patrick smiled. "Accidents happen."

"Let me buy you a new cone," Angela said, picking up the one on the ground and tossing it into the trash.

"You're sure?"

"Please. It's the least I can do."

They went inside, and Patrick ordered the same cone. Angela got a single scoop of dark chocolate, and Jake got a scoop of birthday cake flavor. After grabbing a fistful of napkins, they went back outside. They decided to take a little walk since the benches outside the shop were taken. He'd planned to go into town, get his ice cream, and eat it on his way back home, but the fresh air was clearing his head. It was much better than staring at his computer or gazing at the walls while trying to put words down.

"Are we interrupting your afternoon?" Angela asked.

"No, not at all." Patrick wrapped another napkin around the base of his cone. "I was just getting some fresh air and figured that ice cream could help my writer's block."

"You're a writer? What kinds of things do you write?" She looked much, much more relaxed than she had when they bumped into each other a few weeks back. She had clearly gotten a little sun, and she was dressed much more casually.

"Novels. Usually mystery or suspense. My latest deadline is coming up fast, so I'm a little stressed. It's hard to turn on that creative switch at will, you know?" He shrugged, watching Jake skip a few feet ahead of them.

"Yeah, I get that."

He thought back to when he'd seen her last. "Are you still here on vacation?"

"Nope, not anymore. We're moving back here. Well, Jake and I are. Lydia and I bought that old Beachside Inn down near the water and we're going to update and reopen it."

"Wow, that sounds like a big project. The inn's been shut down for a while."

"It is. We've barely started, but it's already been so rewarding." She caught a drip of ice cream before it ran down her hand. "I'm going through a divorce, so it's nice to have somewhere to focus my thoughts."

Patrick could only nod. He stopped himself from saying that he may be going down that same path soon. He hadn't spoken the word "divorce" aloud, not even to Aubrey. He always said they were "separated" or that they were "taking time apart." Saying "divorce" would make it feel like something too real, something he didn't want to face.

Patrick bit into his cone, taking the opportunity to look at Angela out of the corner of his eye. As much as she sounded excited about the inn, he still heard an undercurrent of sadness in her voice, and he could guess she didn't want to talk about her marriage ending anymore. It had to be a painful subject.

"What are you two planning to do with the inn?" he asked. "Aside from re-opening it, of course."

"There are a lot of repairs, which Lydia is taking the lead on. I'm doing all the decorating." Angela let out a nervous laugh. "I've been an interior decorator for years, and this is by far my biggest project ever."

"I'm sure it'll turn out great. You were always driven and talented in high school, and I doubt that's changed." Patrick shrugged. "I still remember that poetry reading the art club and the literary magazine put on together. That was the best the cafeteria had ever looked. And decorating seems to be your passion, so I'm sure things will be great."

"I can't believe you remember that!" A small smile crossed Angela's lips. "And thanks, Patrick. That's really nice to hear."

"No problem."

A few moments later, Angela came to a stop, calling for Jake. "Well, this is our stop—I need to buy some paint."

"Ah, okay. I should get home and start writing again. Thanks. This helped."

"I'm glad. We'll see you around?" Angela opened the door to the hardware store.

"Yeah, definitely."

Patrick made a loop around the block and headed back toward his house, finishing his cone and pulling his phone out of his pocket. He dialed

Aubrey. He wasn't sure what he was looking for when he called—he was just used to talking with her on walks.

"Hey," he said when Aubrey picked up.

"Hey."

She sounded glad to hear from him, but there was an awkward pause that made Patrick's heart ache. No "hey, babe" or "hey, sweetheart." Just "hey."

"So, how are things?" he asked.

"Fine. My parents are doing well." Aubrey paused again. "How about you?"

"Not bad. I just got some ice cream from The Sweet Creamery to hopefully unfreeze my writer's block." He turned the corner onto their street.

"Did it work?"

"Eh, I think the fresh air did the job a little better, but I don't think I could ever regret ice cream." He chuckled. "I think I should have a fresh mind when I get back to my desk."

There was yet another uncomfortable pause. Conversations between them used to be so easy, sometimes going late into the night. Now they were struggling through small talk.

"I'm going to be home soon. I think we should talk about our future then," Aubrey finally said.

Patrick swallowed, nodding until he remembered that she couldn't see him. "That sounds good."

"All right." She let out a breath. "I'll let you know when I'm on my way back. Good luck with your writing."

"Thanks. Talk soon."

"Bye."

Patrick hung up and unlocked the back door to his house. Despite the lackluster conversation with Aubrey, he *did* feel more up to writing than he had before. He grabbed a glass of water and settled back in at his desk, opening his laptop. Then he let his fingers fly over the keys, inching him closer to finishing the novel.

CHAPTER NINE

"Come in, come in!" Millie said to Angela the moment she opened the magenta door to her house. "Welcome!"

"It's so good to see you!" Angela hugged Millie tight. She hadn't had the chance to spend enough time with the older woman since she and Jake had officially moved to Marigold. "I love what you've done in here!"

Something Angela loved about interior decorating was how people could reflect their own personalities without saying a word. Millie's space was just like the woman herself—vibrant, colorful, and warm. The bold colors of the walls managed to not be overwhelming despite the small space, and the air inside smelled like flowers.

"Thank you!" Millie gently nudged Angela, directing her through the house and toward the back door. "Everyone's out back, if you want to take a look at the rest of the house on the way there. Lydia got here just moments before you did."

Angela went out back, finding Lydia talking to a cluster of women she didn't recognize. Millie had invited several of the women business owners in Marigold over to introduce them to the newest members of their unofficial club.

Angela was relieved and grateful that Millie had offered to connect them with other entrepreneurs in the community. She and Lydia had some support and people to go to for advice. Just looking at the spreadsheets that Lydia had made for them to keep track of their financials had made her head spin. The inn project was a crash course in all things business related.

She had taken one or two business classes in college, but they hardly scratched the surface. Books and blogs could only provide so much information, and they couldn't exactly give you advice. Surely these women would have tips on how to juggle all the parts of running a business.

"There you are!" Lydia jumped up to greet her, then pulled her over to introduce her to the others.

"Angela, this is Leah Rigby, Nicole Howard, and Cora Summers. Leah owns the new hair salon two blocks off Main, Nicole owns that amazing little art gallery that you told me about the other day, and Cora and her husband own the butcher shop that makes those outrageously good sausages you mentioned your mom buying."

"So nice to meet you all!" Angela shook each woman's hand.

If Lydia hadn't told her which woman owned which business, Angela still would have been able to guess what they did. Leah's red hair was perfectly highlighted and shiny, falling past her shoulders. Nicole's outfit screamed artsy and cool in a way that Angela envied. Cora's eyes exuded enthusiasm—she looked like she could tell you everything that you needed to know about making the best steak you'd ever had.

Angela guessed that they were all around her age, though Leah was likely much younger. From the bits and pieces that Millie had told her about everyone before the gathering, Angela could tell that they were the perfect people to talk to.

"I can't believe it's taken us this long to get together," Cora said. "There are so many businesses in town, but I haven't had the chance to really get to know other business owners unless it's by chance."

"I know! And I've been going to your butcher shop at least twice a month since it opened," Nicole said. "Those sausages really are to die for."

Cora smiled, clearly pleased. "Thank you! It's an old family recipe from my husband's grandmother. I knew we had to make it the moment I tasted it. My husband and I love your gallery, by the way."

"Thanks! It feels like a dream to finally have my own business. Sometimes I can hardly believe it."

"Here comes another future business owner." Angela nodded toward the door, where Brooke was coming with a big plate of cookies.

"Who, me?" her sister asked, putting the plate down on the table where Millie had set up some tea and lemonade. "Oh, I'm *years* away from that, if it ever even happens."

"Well, even if it's a few years until you think about starting your own business, it doesn't hurt to talk to other people about running one." Nicole eyed the cookies with interest. "I'm guessing you want to open a bakery? What are these?"

"These are 'everything but the kitchen sink' cookies." Brooke stepped back so everyone could take one. "They have milk chocolate, white chocolate, pretzels, oats, peanuts, and a tiny bit of toffee."

Angela took a bite of hers and closed her eyes. The cookie was perfect and really did have everything—a little salt, a little sweet, a little creamy, a little crunch. All of it came together without being too cloyingly sweet. She grinned to herself as she chewed. Since when had her little sister gotten so good at baking, and why hadn't she started this hobby when everyone lived in the house?

Travis hadn't been kidding when he said that Brooke gave him a batch of cookies more than once a week—now that Lydia, Angela and Jake were in town, Brooke unloaded her creations on them too. The freezer in the innkeeper's residence was stuffed with all sorts of cookies and brownies. Freezing them was the only way they could stop themselves from living on baked goods alone. No one wanted to bite into a cookie that was frozen solid.

Everyone else seemed to be in agreement about how good the cookies were, and the remaining sweet treats started to rapidly disappear. Brooke's face lit up with every compliment she received. Angela hoped it would give her a boost of confidence to go for her dream. Sometimes Brooke needed a little push.

After everyone got their first share of cookies, their conversation easily shifted to business.

"So, how did all of you get established here in Marigold?" Lydia asked.

"Honestly? A lot of it was luck. The right things fell into the right place at the right time," Leah said. "I opened the salon when I was twenty-four and it could have gone so badly. Luckily, I found some great stylists who helped us build a steady clientele."

"Wow, twenty-four?" Angela thought back to being that age. She'd just been starting her career then, and the idea of owning a business would have been laughable to her.

"Leah is the business prodigy of Marigold." Cora grinned, fluffing her cute pixie cut. "Her stylist Simone single-handedly saved me from the terrible bangs I accidentally gave myself."

Everyone laughed.

"I'm far from a prodigy. I've made so many mistakes." Leah took half a cookie from the dwindling pile. "If I hadn't had help from my beauty school mentor and my old boss, I probably would've tanked in the first six months."

"What kinds of mistakes did you make?" Angela asked, reaching into her purse for her notepad. "Do any of you have any advice you wish you had known before you started?"

"Do you have enough space in that notebook? Because I'm sure I've made every mistake in the book," Nicole said jokingly.

Lydia whipped out her notebook too, an eager expression on her face. "We've got the space and the time. Tell us everything."

Everyone was a goldmine of information. Angela and Lydia had already bumped into some of the roadblocks these women had experienced, and now they knew how to get around them. Angela jotted down all the various programs, websites, and contacts that the three other business owners had, making a mental note to reach out to others soon.

The entire evening was fun, relaxing, and informative. Before Angela knew it, she was laughing along with the other business owners like she'd known them for years. She sank back into her seat, feeling like the inn's future looked just a bit brighter than before.

"Where on earth did I put the good tongs?" Lydia murmured to herself, digging through the drawers in the innkeeper's residence's kitchen for what felt like the fiftieth time that hour.

She found them in the last place she thought to look, the drawer next to the ancient dishwasher. She felt settled in, as if she were already putting down roots in Marigold, but there were a few little things that she was still getting used to. The kitchen in the residence was dated, but there was an excellent gas stove and a surprising amount of counter space for such an old home. Plus, there was a nice outdoor space to one side of the residence that she, Angela, and Jake made good use of. Tonight, they were going to eat dinner out there.

She hoped that they had the money to give the kitchen the renovation it desperately needed. She and Angela were doing some smaller things in the residence and inn themselves, like changing hardware and painting, but there was still a lot more to do, and some of it would require professional help.

Lydia pulled the cast-iron skillet from the oven and flipped over the chicken thighs, which were resting on a bed of shallots and bell peppers. She tucked the pan back in and set a timer for another twenty minutes. She'd already taken care of the rest of dinner, so she decided to take the down time to call Holly.

"Hi, Mom!" Her daughter's cheerful voice came through after the second ring. "How are things in Marigold?"

"They're great so far. All this ocean air is making me feel more rested than I have in a while, even with the inn renovations coming up soon."

Lydia filled Holly in on everything that was going on, from the lovely gathering with other women business owners in town to the art that Angela had already arranged to buy from Nicole's gallery for the main sitting area in the inn. It was much quieter on Holly's end of the call than usual, so Lydia was able to hear some plastic clicking against a surface.

"What are you up to, sweet pea?" Lydia asked.

"Just putting on some makeup. I have a date." Holly sounded both nervous and excited, but Lydia only felt her motherly anxiety flare up.

"Oh?" she asked, managing to keep the worry out of her voice. "Who's the lucky guy?"

"His name is Aiden. He was the one who invited everyone out for Thai food a little while back. We've been friends for a while, but he asked me out not long ago."

Lydia remembered his name from one of their

recent calls. "That's great, Hols. What are you two going to do?"

"We're just getting Italian food, so it's not a huge ordeal. But it's an actual date and not one of those vague 'is this a date or not?' situations."

Lydia was relieved that it was a real date. In the other conversations about boys that she and Holly had had in the past, it sounded like all the guys her age didn't know how to express how they felt or what they wanted at all.

"Is he nice?"

"Of course he's nice, Mom. He's seriously one of the nicest guys I've ever met."

"Okay, that's good." Lydia peeked into the oven again to busy herself. Holly hadn't dated steadily in high school—maybe one boy, someone she took to homecoming or prom—so Lydia feared that her daughter would leap into this relationship head first, getting hurt in the process.

"You're totally freaking out, aren't you?" Holly teased, making Lydia laugh.

"A little, but that's my job." She sighed just as the timer went off. "I've gotta go—dinner's ready. It's those chicken thighs and peppers you like."

"Ugh, I wish I could have some. I'm so tired of cafeteria food."

"I'm sure the Italian food will wipe the memory of cafeteria food away, at least for a night. Have a nice time on your date, okay? And I want to hear all about it later. Love you."

"Love you too. Bye."

Lydia hung up and pulled their dinner out of the oven. It smelled amazing—the skin on the chicken thighs had crisped up perfectly, but she could tell the meat underneath was still juicy. She put everything on a platter and took the food to the outdoor dining table just as Angela and Jake walked up. To Lydia's surprise, Grant was with them. He still had that serious look on his face, and he was wearing a flannel shirt buttoned up over a t-shirt, like he had been working outside.

"Look who we found on our walk!" Angela said, putting a hand on Grant's shoulder.

Lydia deflated a tiny bit but maintained her composure. Grant nodded at her in greeting. She couldn't tell if he was angry or disappointed about them getting the inn instead of him. He couldn't be *that* upset if Angela had roped him into coming along with her, could he?

Either way, Lydia was still annoyed at him from their conversation at the open house. Their idea to reopen the inn wasn't stupid at all, no matter what he thought.

"Do you mind if he stays for dinner?" Angela asked.

"Sure, no problem." Lydia made herself smile. She couldn't exactly say no at this point without coming across as incredibly rude. "There's enough to go around."

They all settled around the table and dished up the food. The recipe she'd made didn't really have a specific name, but Lydia cooked it often because it combined some of her favorite foods: chicken thighs, roasted bell peppers and shallots, and a creamy cauliflower mash that was so good that Jake ate it without even realizing he was eating his veggies.

"Wow, this is delicious," Grant said after he took his first bite, sounding surprised. "What's it called?"

"It doesn't really have a name. It's just something I make pretty often because it's simple and tastes good after a long day." Lydia's cheeks flushed at Grant's compliment. "It's a family favorite."

"It's great." He scooped a few more bell peppers onto his plate.

"Where did you guys bump into each other?" Lydia asked.

"On the beach. I live not too far from here,

maybe a half mile or so." Grant sat back in his seat, taking a sip of his wine. "I was just taking an evening walk, trying to decide what to eat for dinner. Angela was kind enough to invite me."

"Oh, so we're neighbors." Lydia wasn't sure how she felt about that. Would she have to look over her shoulder every time she took a walk on the beach to avoid an embarrassing moment like the first time they saw each other? Or would she bump into him all the time and have little arguments?

"That we are."

He looked at her with an expression Lydia couldn't quite read. He *looked* grumpy, but the words that were coming out of his mouth didn't sound that way. Lydia wasn't sure which one she could trust.

The topic shifted over to Jake's new school, which he loved. He already had play dates lined up with a few other kids, and he was enjoying his social studies class. His entire class had thrown a big party for everyone born in the spring earlier in the week, and Angela had sent him to school with some of Brooke's colorful Funfetti cookies. Like literally everything Brooke baked, it was a huge hit with the kids.

"Mommy, can we have some cookies for

dessert?" Jake asked, pointing at where his cauliflower mash used to be. "I ate all my veggies."

"Of course, hon. Why don't you run and grab some for all of us?" Angela smiled.

Jake ran inside like he was being chased, making the adults laugh.

"Some days, I wish I had a tenth of the energy he has." Angela shook her head fondly, finishing the rest of her white wine.

"Energy's wasted on the young, isn't it?" Lydia glanced over her shoulder at the door. "Looking back, I'm surprised I could keep up with Holly at all. I guess I was pretty young back then too."

"Is Holly your daughter?" Grant asked.

"Mm-hm. She's in college now at Syracuse University."

Grant nodded. "Good school."

"It is. She loves it."

They sat in comfortable silence, and Lydia studied Grant out of the corner of her eye. The more she talked to him, the more curious she was to know his story. How long had he been on Marigold? What had brought him here?

"Um, Mommy?" Jake said, coming through the back door with the plate of cookies. His foot squished with a damp sound inside his shoe. "I think something's wrong. The floor is really wet in the kitchen."

Angela and Lydia looked at each other, wide-eyed. Then, without a word, they both leapt up from the table and raced toward the house.

CHAPTER TEN

Grant watched Lydia and Angela leap to their feet and rush into the house, the relaxed energy from a moment ago evaporating in an instant. He followed, and sure enough, there was water all over the old kitchen's floor.

They scanned the kitchen with frantic energy, trying to see where the water was coming from. It wasn't gushing out in a torrent, but it had clearly been leaking from somewhere at a steady pace. The water was creeping closer and closer to the carpeted living space. If it hit the old carpet, the problem would get even worse.

"Ah, I can't believe this. How long has this been happening?" Lydia grimaced, walking gingerly through the puddled water so she could get closer to the leak's probable source. "How on earth did I miss this when I was cooking? Have we been eating dinner for that long?"

"You were busy, and I doubt the leak announced itself loudly," Angela said, heaving a sigh and grabbing a bunch of towels from a nearby closet. "The inspector did say the plumbing was getting a little worn down in here, though it likely wouldn't be a priority."

"It is now." Lydia ran a hand through her brown hair, her brows furrowed.

"I guess this is what we get with an old house, huh?" Angela looked equally frustrated, and worry burned in her blue eyes as well.

"True. That doesn't make it any easier to deal with, though." Lydia opened the cabinet under the sink, peering inside. "At least it's an easily accessible pipe for the most part. But I have no idea how to fix this, and I'm sure there aren't any plumbers on the island who are working this late."

"I can take a look at it. It might be easier to fix than you think," Grant offered. He tiptoed through the water to check, ducking his head to look under the sink. From the look of things, it would be a simple enough fix. "Yeah, I can do this if you guys have a basic tool kit. I should be able to get it patched up fast."

Lydia sagged in relief. "Really?"

"Yep, it's no problem."

"I'm pretty sure my parents have a shop vac to dry up all this water. There aren't enough towels in this place to soak this water up any time soon." Angela pulled out her phone and started texting someone. "I'll go pick it up right now."

"That sounds perfect." Lydia stepped out of the puddle of water. "Let me go grab the kit."

Angela and Jake took off to her parents' house while Lydia went to grab the kit. Grant rolled up his sleeves and grabbed a couple of the towels Angela had left on the counter just so they'd have a little area to kneel down without getting too wet.

"Here's the kit. I hope it has what you need." Lydia returned and handed him a medium-sized tool box.

"It should. I'll need you to hand me some things, though." Grant opened the toolkit and pulled out the flashlight first. "Could you hold this for me?"

Lydia did as he asked, angling the flashlight to light up the pipes, and Grant got to work. He temporarily stopped the flood of water with a few turns of his wrench. That was the easy part—now he had to make sure it stayed. He worked quietly, asking Lydia to move the flashlight from time to time or hand him something.

"Wow, how'd you learn how to do all this?" Lydia asked as Grant fiddled with the pipes a little more.

He shrugged. "I was always the handyman at our house."

"Oh." He could hear the surprise in her voice. "I didn't realize you were married."

Grant grimaced, swapping his wrench for some pliers. He hadn't intended to bring his late wife up, and now they'd have to have the awkward conversation people always had when dealing with grief—stilted apologies, uncomfortable silences, and pitying looks. He still hadn't gotten used to those moments, even two years after Annie's death.

"I'm not," he said. "I mean, I was, but my wife passed away about two years ago."

With those words, he dipped back under the sink to tighten a joint that was already tight enough, hoping Lydia would leave the subject alone.

* * *

Lydia watched Grant duck beneath the sink, getting the sense he was hiding from her a bit by focusing on the task at hand. She completely understood that impulse. The condolences from people, no matter how well meaning, got a little exhausting after a while. Grief was lonely, even if you had people around.

"I'm sorry," she offered, her voice simple and sincere. "My husband passed away too. About a year ago, of cancer."

Grant popped his head out from under the sink again, looking at her with surprise in his eyes.

"I'm sorry," he said quietly. "I know you've probably gotten a lot of apologies too."

"I have. It's always hard to know what to say in these instances. Saying 'I'm sorry for your loss' never feels like enough, but you don't want to stay silent." Lydia switched the flashlight to her other hand. "I don't blame people for trying."

"True." He looked back at what he was doing, then glanced back up at her. "Could you hand me that smaller wrench, please?"

Lydia handed it over. After considering for a moment, she said, "That night when you first saw me on the beach? I was talking to him. His name was Paul. I don't know why I do it—talk to him as if he can still hear me—but I haven't stopped even after a year."

Grant sat back and looked at her. His expression was still as serious as ever, but there seemed to be slightly less tension around his eyes and mouth than before. Lydia thought it made him look a bit younger, a bit softer. She felt like he was seeing who she really was, at least for a brief moment.

"I do that too. In fact, I did it that night we bumped into each other." He shrugged. "It's not the best solution, but sometimes it just feels comforting."

Lydia nodded, feeling less crazy than she had in a while. It helped to talk to someone else who knew what grief felt like, and how even nonsensical things sometimes helped make the tough days a little easier. "Yeah, comforting is the right word. I don't think I've told anyone about doing it, not even Angela."

"I haven't told anyone either. I don't think they'd get it unless they've been through it." Grant put his tools down, straightening up. "It's hard to explain how everything you do can make you miss a person, even something as simple as washing your hands."

"God, I know." Lydia clicked off the flashlight to save its battery. "It's still hard for me to load the dishwasher. That was Paul's job. I hated doing it before, but now it's worse. It's not about the dishes—it's about the reminder of him."

"I hate that too. I haven't watched a single baseball game since Annie died. I was never into it when we first met, but she was. Eventually, she converted me, but now I can't stand the idea of yelling at the TV alone." Grant huffed a small laugh, though it didn't reach his eyes.

"It's so hard."

"It really is." He shook his head slightly, a faraway look coming into his eyes. "And it'll always be there, that pain."

Lydia felt the tiniest bit of weight come off her shoulders. People always told her that talking about her pain, whether it was in therapy or some sort of support group, would help, but part of her didn't believe it. But just talking to Grant, a man she'd been on the fence about not two hours earlier, made her feel more understood than she had in a long time.

"How have you coped, besides mostly one-sided conversations?" Lydia asked.

"Mm, different ways."

Leaning against the counter, Grant told her about going for walks, playing with dogs at the local shelter, and walking downtown when he felt lonely, and Lydia told him how her relationship with Holly had kept her going. They chatted, sometimes tweaking the pipes but mostly talking. Lydia jumped when she heard the sound of little feet running through the house.

"We got the big vacuum!" Jake announced, coming to a skidding stop in the doorway.

"We did! It should make cleaning up super easy," Angela said, rolling the shop vac behind her.

The Grant that Lydia had gotten to know over their brief time alone shuttered himself away, and his rugged face went back to its normal gruff default. He ducked back underneath the sink, tweaked a few final things, then sat back up.

"That should hold the leak for now," Grant said, standing. "I suggest calling a real plumber in as soon as you can, just to make sure things are okay with the other pipes."

"You're such a lifesaver. Thank you!" Angela said.

"Seriously, thanks," Lydia added. "I don't know what we would have done without you."

"Not a problem. Thanks for all the delicious food."

"I'll walk you out. Take a cookie for the road."

Lydia slipped some cookies into a bag and led Grant out toward the beach. When they reached the soft sand, he nodded a goodbye and headed along the waterfront toward his home.

Lydia watched his back as his form got smaller and smaller as he walked away. She was strangely sad to see him go. She'd seen a whole new side of him, one that she liked more than she ever would have guessed.

CHAPTER ELEVEN

Angela inhaled, letting the salty morning air fill her lungs, and exhaled. She and Brooke had started meeting up for a morning walk every once in a while, and it was one of the best things she had done to de-stress. It was especially nice now that it was late April and the weather was really starting to warm up.

She was waiting for Brooke to arrive, having gotten up a few minutes before her alarm this morning.

After the pipe leak incident a week ago, Angela had realized she was more tightly wound than she'd thought she was. She wasn't the type to have meltdowns, but the worry and stress had nearly sent her over the edge. Then she'd spent half the night tossing and turning, worrying about other pipes exploding in the night.

Walking on the beach first thing in the morning, talking about life with her younger sister, was a great way to relax and slow her mind down a little. The two women had always gotten along well, but with Angela in Philadelphia and Brooke in Marigold, they'd grown apart a little in recent years. Now that they were both living in the same place, they could get close again, especially since they were both adults now. The last time Angela had lived in Marigold, their seven-year age difference had felt massive. Now they could relate to each other much more.

"Hey, hey!" Brooke said, waving at Angela as she approached from the small parking lot near the inn. "Good morning."

"Morning!" Angela hugged her sister. "Ready?"

"Sure thing."

The two women headed out along the beach. They walked quietly for a few minutes, with only the sounds of the birds and the ocean filling the air between them.

"I had the weirdest stress dream last night," Angela said after a while. "Scott wouldn't leave me alone until I'd made him enough spaghetti for ten people in this tiny little pot. He kept pleading for it over and over again like he hadn't eaten in a month. I don't even think he likes spaghetti all that much."

Brooke laughed. "What on earth? That's so strange! I wonder what it means."

"I know, it really was odd. It's probably my brain trying to tell me something in its own weird way." Angela sighed. "It's just the divorce, probably. It's been on my mind a lot lately."

"How is that going?"

"Slow. I thought I would be one of the lucky ones who got it over with quickly, especially since Scott seemed to be willing to go through with it. But now he's dragging his feet and taking a century to answer emails or calls."

"Ah." Brooke wrinkled her nose in irritation.

"I know." Angela stooped to pick up a seashell and turned it over in her hands. "He wants to come to Marigold to visit and really show me that he can be better."

"Will you let him come? Do you even want to give him a second chance?"

Angela paused, considering her sister's question. Would seeing Scott in a relatively closed environment really prove anything? The woman he'd had an affair with was someone who worked in the same office building as he did, so he saw her all the time. And most of his interactions with her had been far outside of Angela's view.

She doubted he would start a different affair if he came to the island to prove he could be a better husband—but that didn't mean he wouldn't stray again once their lives went back to normal in Philly if she agreed to get back together with him. His visit wouldn't really prove anything significant.

But then again, she and Scott had been together for thirteen years. That meant something. He was a good, loving father to Jake, too. She'd noticed Jake asking about his dad a little more often as of late and still wasn't sure how to talk to him about the whole mess.

She sighed. "I think I owe it to Jake to give Scott a chance. Or at least, that's what I've been thinking. I don't think I should rob him of the opportunity to have his dad around all the time and not just on the weekends."

As she finished speaking Angela tossed the shell she had been fiddling with into the water.

Brooke didn't say anything in response, though Angela could tell her sister was skeptical, and rightfully so. Brooke had liked Scott before, but now, like the rest of the Collins family, she didn't like him at all. But instead of pushing it, Brooke stayed quiet.

"Hey, so I've been thinking more about baking for the inn," she said instead, changing the subject. "I think it would be a great first step toward opening a bakery of my own someday. A way to practice and get my feet wet. When I talked to Cora at that gathering Millie had, she told me about how she and her husband started at the farmer's market before leaping to a storefront. That sounds so much more do-able, you know?"

"That's an amazing idea."

Angela was pleasantly surprised that Brooke was taking active steps toward being a part of the inn. Brooke tended to float from interest to interest, not always finishing what she set out to do. She had changed her major at least four times, bouncing from biology to English to anthropology before sticking with English once and for all. Seeing her motivated to really get her baking career off the ground was fantastic.

"I hoped you'd think so." Brooke grinned. "I kind of needed your permission."

"You think I'd turn down your treats? The only reason I would ever do that is if we ran out of space entirely in our freezer." Angela linked her arm in

Brooke's, just like they'd done when they were kids. "Tell me more about what you're thinking of selling."

Brooke excitedly told Angela about her vision for the inn's mini bakery. Angela's mouth watered at the idea of Brooke's crumbly, buttery scones and light, delicious blueberry muffins.

It would be a perfect fit, and Angela couldn't wait to mesh her sister's dreams with her own.

Lydia didn't know of any other way to put it: the inn was a total mess. There were buckets of paint everywhere, half-demolished walls where the contractor was updating the heating system, and one entire room had half-carpet and half old, beat-up wood floors. And that wasn't even counting the dust or the furniture that had been pushed wherever it would fit.

But it was okay—it wasn't going to look amazing in a day. It was a work in progress, and the progress was steadily chugging along.

Lydia pushed open one of the windows on the first floor a little wider and turned up her music. The downstairs bedrooms needed the least amount of work to get them in shape. The hardwood had already been refinished, so now the bedroom just needed a fresh coat of paint. Lydia loved the color Angela had chosen for this room, a soothing sage green.

While Angela was out hunting for antiques and other pieces of furniture, Lydia kept herself busy with the things she was able to do on her own. She picked up a paint roller and dipped it into the paint, running it up the walls while humming along to her music. The sun hit the first layer of paint, making the color look even better. Lydia grinned to herself. Angela was seriously good at her job. The color was absolutely lovely.

The song changed to something more upbeat, and between her good mood and the rhythm of the music, Lydia couldn't help but shake her hips a little.

She turned to refill her pan of paint and jumped, spotting someone standing in the doorway. It was Grant, leaning against the doorframe.

He looked much more amused than she had ever seen him, a genuine smile curving his lips. Her cheeks flushed from more than just embarrassment as she took in his expression. The skin around his brown eyes crinkled a little, and Lydia could see the tiniest hint of a dimple under his stubble. It made him look like the Grant she'd gotten to know while he fixed the pipes—softer, and admittedly, very attractive.

"Do you sneak into people's houses often?" she asked with a little laugh.

"The front door was open." He shrugged. Lydia realized she must have left it open when she was lugging in all the paint. "And it's an inn, not a house. It's a little less weird if you think of it that way."

Lydia grinned, feeling warmth spread through her belly. Hearing him call it an inn made all of this feel even more real. Especially after he'd seemed so down on the idea at the open house.

"That's true. It would be hard to rent a room at an inn if the doors were locked all the time." Lydia picked up the paint can again and poured some of the viscous liquid into her pan. "What brought you in?"

"I was just in the area and wondered if you needed help."

That was one of the last things Lydia had expected him to say, and her eyebrows shot up. She couldn't help the smile that spread across her face. Even though Grant wasn't a huge fan of keeping the inn as it was, he was still willing to help.

"Oh! Thank you. That's really nice of you." She paused. "You're sure you have time for this? What about your business? I don't know anything about landscaping, so excuse me if this is a dumb question."

He had mentioned that he owned a small landscaping business the night the sink pipes had leaked, but she hadn't gotten many more details than that.

"It's not a dumb question at all." He looked around the messy room. "Yeah, I have the time. My guys have smaller projects that they can easily handle today—yard trimming, basic flower beds, things like that. I finished up all the management stuff I had to do, so I'm totally free."

"Okay, then. I would really appreciate your help." She leaned over and grabbed a fresh roller. "I'm just painting, and having you here will make this go even faster. Thank you, seriously."

"No problem at all." He took the roller and followed her lead, starting on the adjacent wall that had already been sectioned off with painter's tape.

Lydia started painting her wall again, glancing over her shoulder at Grant from time to time, just to make sure she wasn't imagining things. She was grateful for his help since this room was bigger than the others, but she still couldn't believe he dropped by just to help out.

Grant seemed to be full of surprises.

CHAPTER TWELVE

Angela gave the porch some solid stomps with her foot, not worrying that it would cave in like she had every time she'd walked into the inn before. The porch was freshly remodeled—the contractors had reinforced the wood to stabilize the saggy areas and had completely redone the stairs leading up to it.

Angela and Lydia had painted it white, which would go perfectly with the furniture Angela had gotten for a steal at the antiques store. It already looked inviting without the furniture, but once it was all set up outside, guests would be clamoring to stop by. Or at least, Angela hoped they would.

She looked around the porch one more time before heading in. Over the past few weeks, the changes to the inn had really started coming together. The floors were refinished, most of the walls were painted, and the updated light fixtures were in place. Some of the decor was waiting to be put up on the walls or onto furniture, but she was still working on that.

She grabbed a pitcher of peach iced tea from the fridge, plus a few glasses, and headed to the room in the back where they'd set up a makeshift workspace. Lydia was sitting at the table behind her laptop, keeping an eye on Jake as he kicked around a soccer ball in the yard.

"Still looking over the spreadsheets?" Angela asked, putting the tea down.

"Yep." Lydia sat back in her seat and stretched her arms into the air. "I've got the budget and the schedule open. We're actually on track with the schedule, which is awesome, but the budget is getting a little tight."

Angela came around to look over Lydia's shoulder. Spreadsheets weren't as intimidating anymore, especially since Angela had been talking to some of the other business owners she'd met at Millie's, but they still weren't her favorite thing to look over. Some of the repairs had cost slightly more than they'd budgeted, but they'd also spent a little less on some of the decor by buying gently used antiques and rehabbing them.

"We need to start bringing money in, fast." Angela sat on the other side of the table. "With all the big repairs done, I think we can do it."

"Yeah, I think so too." Lydia clicked around a little, then turned the laptop so they could both see it. "Our web designer finished up the inn's site, by the way. It looks amazing."

Millie had hooked them up with a young Marigold couple, Thom and Anita, who were just starting their web development and design business. Wanting to support fellow Marigold businesses, Angela and Lydia had gone to them to put together the inn's website. It was perfect. Angela had taken a few photography classes over the years, so she'd taken photos of the beach around the inn and a few of the rooms that she'd staged just for the site.

Even the website's design captured the charm that the inn itself had, with some modern touches. Guests would be able to put in requests for rooms online, and once everything was set up, they would be able to go on a virtual tour to take a peek at all the rooms available. They'd written up a brief history of the inn and of Marigold as an added touch.

"It looks so, so good." Angela clapped her hands

together. "I'm so glad Millie put us in touch with Thom and Anita."

"Right? Millie's like a human business database for the island." Lydia chuckled as she took a sip of tea. "We should pick an opening day and have that added to the site."

Lydia pulled up their schedule spreadsheet again, as well as a calendar. The biggest priority was making the inn safe to be in, which they'd mostly handled, and having enough furniture for people to be comfortable. Angela had ordered some custom work on some of the beds and pieces for the common area, and the contractors were going to finish up the bathroom tiling and cabinet hardware soon.

"This is aggressive, but what if we set the opening day for two weeks before the Summer Sand Festival?" Lydia asked.

"Wow." Angela blinked. "That's in mid-July. It's coming up fast. But it does sound perfect. People will be coming onto the island throughout the whole week of the festival, and we're not too far from where a lot of the events will take place."

"I think we can do it." Lydia had the determined look in her eye that Angela had gotten well acquainted with over the past several weeks. "It'll be hard, but things have been going great so far."

"Yeah, let's go for it." Angela raised her hand, and Lydia met it in a high five. "Do you want some celebratory lunch? I'm kind of in the mood for chicken salad sandwiches for some reason."

"I'm always down for celebratory food." Lydia typed a last few notes in and closed her laptop. "Grant should be here any minute, though, if you don't mind waiting for him."

"Oh?"

Right on time, they heard footsteps coming through the inn. Grant had been coming by a lot to help Lydia with painting and doing small cosmetic repairs, so they were used to him coming and going.

"Hey, there." Grant nodding in greeting as he stepped into the room.

"Hey, glad you're here." Lydia stood, smoothing her casual t-shirt dress. "We were just about to eat lunch—would you like something?"

"That would be great, thanks." Grant wasn't the most smiley guy, but he gave Lydia a half-smile that reached his brown eyes, making them warm.

"We're having chicken salad sandwiches, probably, and whatever else we can whip up on the side." Lydia smiled back. "If that sounds good."

"Absolutely. Everything I've eaten here has been great, so I know this will be too."

"I'll go get it started since it was my idea," Angela said, excusing herself to the kitchen.

She started putting together the chicken salad from ingredients they already had in the fridge, starting with some poached chicken breasts that she cut into medium-sized chunks. She listened in on Lydia and Grant's conversation as she worked, folding some tarragon and parsley that Millie had grown in her garden into the salad.

Angela heard Lydia laugh from time to time and gathered that they were talking about Grant's landscaping business. He'd started it with a business partner years ago, and now it sounded like it was thriving. They were going to do some landscaping for the inn, too.

Angela finished making the sandwiches and paired them with some crunchy kettle chips from Nature's Way Market. They featured a lot of handmade foods from small businesses in the region and these chips had become a favorite of hers. She called Jake inside, and they all sat around the slightly larger table in the unfinished dining room to eat.

The conversation flowed easily, mostly between Lydia and Grant. Grant entertained them with stories of the most elaborate landscaping jobs he'd ever done—which were more plentiful than Angela would have ever guessed—speaking in that serious, gruff voice of his. But despite his tone, Angela could hear a lightness to his voice that she hadn't heard when they'd first met.

Once they finished lunch, Angela decided to take Jake down to the beach to fly some kites. He had gotten used to running around outside, so now they went out to the beach all the time.

"We'll probably be back in an hour or two," Angela said as she slipped on her sunglasses.

"Sounds good." Lydia glanced at Grant. "We're just going to paint one of the last bedrooms while you're out—the one with that beautiful blue-gray shade you chose."

"All right. I'm excited to see it!" Angela turned to Jake. "Ready to go, buddy?"

"Yes!" Jake nodded and ran off toward the car.

Angela chuckled, gathering her purse. She looked over her shoulder to where Grant and Lydia were grabbing some supplies. Grant lightly touched Lydia on her arm as they headed toward the room they needed to paint. Both of them were smiling a little.

She knew that Lydia and Grant hadn't gotten off on the right foot at all. She'd heard their snippy conversation on the way down the stairs during the open house. Lydia was never that sassy to anyone, so Grant must have set her off. On top of that, they had beaten Grant's offer on the inn. If she hadn't run into him on the beach and brought him over, she doubted that Lydia would have reached out to him.

But now they were talking enthusiastically, laughing like old friends. Angela wondered what had changed and mentally filed that question for Lydia away.

Am I imagining something between them? Angela thought as she walked to the car. *Or is there something there?*

* * *

Gazing out at the water sometimes helped Patrick get over smaller bouts of writer's block, which was why he'd come down to the boardwalk to work. But the change in scenery still wasn't helping him get into the groove.

He deleted a line of dialogue he'd written with a heavy sigh. Nothing sounded right to him.

The newly opened casual snack bar where he was sitting had Wi-Fi and a lot of outdoor seating, so he wasn't the only person on a laptop at this time of day. He wondered if anyone else was struggling as much as he was.

He opened his email against his better judgment, only to find a message from his editor asking how the book was coming along. Patrick sipped his lemonade and debated how to respond. Going the honest route might make his editor panic and debate whether to push back his release date, which Patrick didn't want to deal with. He typed a few responses before deleting all of them, taking a more neutral road.

It's going well—excited for you to see it.

He hit send before he could stop himself. Maybe if he put that optimism out into the universe, it would magically come true.

He went back to his draft for a few moments, getting a few sentences down before his attention drifted again. It was a breezy day, so there were a lot of people flying kites on the beach. He spotted Angela and Jake, running back and forth as they tried to get their kite airborne. It dipped and swerved until it finally caught a breeze, making Jake jump around in excitement.

Patrick smiled, even though the sight made his chest ache. Aubrey had always known that kids weren't for her—she was more interested in her career and in being an aunt to her sister's two kids.

He'd always thought he would be fine being the fun uncle and growing old with just her in the house.

Now, he wasn't so sure. Part of him still wanted a family to fill his home.

But he'd made a commitment to Aubrey, which meant that the desire for kids had taken a back seat. He wouldn't dream of pushing an idea on her that she was openly against, especially because she would be the one who would have to carry the child if they decided to have one of their own. And the adoption process was a difficult one, too, if they went that route.

He glanced back down at his phone for a moment, pulling up his texts. Aubrey had texted him her travel itinerary the other day, since she had decided to come home soon. He hoped they could work things out. He still wasn't any closer to figuring out any viable solution. They'd seen a marriage counselor for a while, but it hadn't smoothed over the issues in their relationship. All it had done was made them realize that they wanted completely different things.

He wondered what Aubrey had thought about in her time away. Had she been mulling all of this over as intently as he was?

Hopefully, they'd be able to move forward in

some direction once she got back—either together or separately. The idea that his marriage might be ending still hurt, but this in-between place felt almost worse. At least once they both decided what they really wanted, they would have some certainty and closure on the matter.

Angela looked up, her eyes connecting with Patrick's when he glanced toward the beach again. She gave a small wave as she recognized him. Patrick waved back and watched her and Jake come up the beach and across the boardwalk.

"Hey!" Angela said. She had clearly gotten some sun, and so had Jake, making their blonde hair seem brighter. "Working away?"

"More or less." Patrick smiled. "I like to leave the house to write when things aren't going smoothly, but today I've been looking at the water for the most part."

"You're writing stories?" Jake asked, his eyes wide. "About what?"

If Patrick had to guess, Jake was probably around five or six. That meant Jake was a little over ten years too young to read the books he'd written. Patrick glanced up at Angela for a moment before deciding to tell her little boy the PG version.

"Yep, I'm writing a novel. It's a mystery—a

detective is trying to find someone who hurt a lot of people before a big hurricane hits and washes away the evidence."

"Wow..." Jake looked at Patrick like he was a rock star. "A whole book?"

"A whole book." Patrick nodded, smiling.

He remembered the first time he'd met an author when he was just a few years older than Jake. It had blown his mind to learn that people could write stories for a living. Ever since he'd learned how to read, he had written little stories of his own. Once he knew that he could do his favorite thing all day, he hadn't stopped writing.

"Jake's always had a big imagination, and he loves stories," Angela said with a smile. Jake opened his mouth to ask another question, but Angela rested her hand on his head. "We better let Patrick get back to work, buddy."

"It was nice bumping into you," Patrick said.

"Likewise!"

Angela smiled over her shoulder and steered Jake back toward the beach. As they walked away, Patrick could hear Jake rattling off question after question. He turned back to his manuscript and instantly found the flow he'd been searching for all day.

CHAPTER THIRTEEN

Grant ducked his head as he followed Lydia down the stairs into the basement of the Beachside Inn.

"I really hope there aren't any spiders in here," Lydia said, flicking on the light switch that sat on one wall. "Angela went down here the other day and cleared out some cobwebs, but she's never been scared of bugs."

Lydia clearly was. The old inn had come with a few residents, namely a few insects here and there. Grant had been the designated spider remover during the renovations. He didn't mind—he wouldn't have gotten into landscaping if he was scared of a few critters.

"I'm sure it'll be okay. I'd avoid putting my hand into dark boxes, though," Grant said with a chuckle.

He looked across the basement. It was cluttered, with stacks of old boxes, broken pieces of furniture, and other random items scattered about. It smelled a little dusty, but it didn't have the damp smell that signaled water leakage. Once they cleared it out, there would be plenty of space to make a more organized storage area.

Lydia put her hands on her hips, glancing around. "Let's put all the broken furniture or obvious trash over to my left, then all the stuff we want to sort through on the right."

"Sounds like a good plan."

They started with the more obvious trash—outdated electronics, empty boxes, broken tools. Then they started in on the boxes. Lydia found several small figurines and vases that could be revamped, along with paperwork that she wanted to go through later. Grant mostly found old newspapers, beach gear that someone could probably use, and clothing or shoes that guests must have left behind.

"Oh, cool—look at these." Lydia waved Grant over to a box she'd just opened. "They're old photos of the inn! These would be great for the walls in the entryway. And for the website, too."

Grant looked over her shoulder at the faded

pictures, which likely spanned a few decades. There were beautiful photos of the waterfront and the old buildings that had been repurposed for newer businesses recently. Guests appeared in some of them, laughing around bonfires, sitting on the beach with their arms around each other's shoulders, or relaxing on the front porch.

"Wait, hold on." Grant took a photo that Lydia had gone past quickly from the stack. "Is this *you*?"

Lydia studied it, then blinked. "Oh, wow, it is!"

The younger version of Lydia had the same brown hair, but it was cut in a way that had been stylish two decades ago. She was sitting on a picnic blanket on the beach at sunset, next to a man and a woman who looked like her parents. All of them were grinning widely, squeezed close together to fit in the frame. There was a genuine closeness between them that even a still photo could pick up.

Grant looked up at Lydia, whose eyes had grown misty. She blinked, clearing her throat as she tucked the photos gently into the "save" box. Grant gazed at the picture, which was still on top. Lydia looked so sweet and happy in the photo, as if nothing in the world could bring her down.

"You must have been having a good time," he said softly.

"Yeah, I was. I don't remember the exact day that picture was taken, but I remember so many like it. So many amazing memories." Lydia stopped working on the next box. Her gaze fell somewhere past his head, like she was looking into the past. "That's why this place matters so much to me. It looks like just an inn, but it's more than that. Something about the energy and all the fun I had with my parents and my friends made it magical, almost. Once we get it up and running, we can give that to other families, too."

Grant smiled, unable to stop himself. She said the words with such conviction that he wondered why he'd ever doubted her idea to update the place. Lydia threw herself wholeheartedly into every single thing they worked on together, whether it was painting a baseboard or tightening a screw. If anyone was going to make the inn shine again, it would be her and Angela. He knew they would make this inn someone's special memory in the very near future.

"Hey, come with me. I want to show you something," he said, closing up the box he was working on. He knew just the place to take Lydia—a place with his own special memories. They had been working all day, and they needed a proper break.

"Right now?" Lydia laughed, looking at the still-full basement. They'd hardly made a dent. In fact, it looked a little worse because of all the things they were getting rid of, stacked up on the floor.

"Right now." Grant took his first step onto the stairs, turning back to look at her over his shoulder. "It'll be here tomorrow for us to finish. It's not like any of this is immediately in anyone's way. Will you come? I promise it'll be worth it. All you'll need is your sneakers and maybe a bottle of water."

Lydia paused, her hands on the box and her bottom lip between her teeth. Then she nodded, a smile breaking out on her face.

"Sure, let's go."

Lydia inhaled deeply as they drove across the island in Grant's car, the breeze stirring her hair through the open windows. The radio was on, but that was the only sound between them. She glanced at Grant when he wasn't paying attention, curiosity rising inside her.

Where was he taking her? He seemed excited about it, so she guessed it was someplace special. But why now?

And why had she dropped everything to go somewhere with him on a complete whim? That wasn't like her. She was a finisher—nothing was ever left half-done, even temporarily and even if the temptation of fun was calling her name. In college, she'd never pulled a single all-nighter because procrastinating wasn't in her vocabulary. She created plans and followed through as written.

But leaving something for later felt good—right, even. She hadn't had anyone pull her out of her intense focus since Paul. *Let's live a little, Lyds*, was what he'd always said.

Going on a spontaneous ride when she still had a lot of things on her to-do list surely counted as living, especially when it was with someone like Grant. He could be surprisingly easy going, but he didn't seem like the type to do this either.

She glanced over at Grant again as he made a left turn, taking them toward the far end of the island, and he looked back at her.

"It's not far now," he promised.

He drove for another two or three minutes, then pulled into a parking lot near the bluffs and a walking trail. There were a few cars here and there, mostly tourists from what Lydia could tell. She had never been over here before, even though she always enjoyed a good walk.

They hiked in comfortable silence up a dirt trail,

ending at the edge of the bluffs overlooking the ocean. The grass was overgrown here, growing into the path they'd walked up on. They'd passed other hikers on their walk up, but no one was around now.

Neither of them broke the comfortable, easy silence between them. There was only the sound of the waves crashing against the rocks below, and the occasional call from birds.

They kept walking until they reached a nice bench to sit on and look out onto the ocean. The breeze was more intense up here, and Lydia was only wearing a t-shirt and shorts. She scooted a little closer to Grant's body heat, and he didn't move away from her.

"Sorry, I should have told you to bring a sweatshirt," he said. "I forgot how much cooler it can be up here."

"It's okay. The view is worth it. I can't believe I've never been up here before."

"I can't believe it either. We both know how you feel about views of the water." Grant nudged her with his shoulder, clearly teasing.

"Hey!" Lydia snorted and smiled. It had become a running joke between them since he kept catching her staring off into the horizon whenever she had anything important on her mind.

They fell back into silence, watching a flock of birds go by, and she stole another glance at the man beside her.

How had he known that this was exactly what she needed?

Even *she* hadn't realized how much she had been running herself to the bone. She told herself that she was unwinding enough at night by cooking dinner or having a glass of wine, but she hadn't done anything like this in ages. She took a deep breath of clean air and let it out.

She really liked Grant's company. Even if they worked on something in the inn all day, she never got tired of him. He knew just when to pull back and just when Lydia needed a little distracting. And apparently, he could tell when she needed an even bigger break like this. She hoped he felt the same way about her. It seemed like he did, at least. He kept coming by and he was always ready to help.

"I almost left Marigold after Annie died," Grant said suddenly, his eyes trained on the horizon. "But in the end, I couldn't do it. It's my home, even though some of the memories I have are painful. I wasn't even expecting to like it when we moved here, but I love it."

"I do too. I've only been here a little while, but

it's hard to imagine going back to my old life once the inn is open and stable." Lydia picked at a piece of dry grass that was so overgrown she could touch it without leaning down. "I don't think everyone's suited to the slower pace here, but I think I am. I hardly realized how much Boston was wearing on me until it wasn't."

"Well, I'm glad you came here." He gently bumped his shoulder against hers again.

Lydia finally looked up to him, surprised at how close their faces were. She was even more surprised at the overwhelming urge she had to kiss him. She hadn't kissed anyone since Paul's death, and she hadn't wanted to until now. She forgot how much the parts before a kiss were just as nerve-wracking as the idea of the kiss itself.

His lips looked soft, and when their gazes locked, she was entranced by the lighter, almost golden flecks in his brown irises. Grant wasn't moving either, and the air between them felt thick with anticipation. She leaned in a little, feeling her heart pound hard in her chest. Just a few more inches would close the gap, erasing the last bit of space between them.

But before their lips could meet, her phone buzzed in her pocket, making them both jump apart.

Lydia fumbled around until she finally pulled it out. When she looked at the screen, her heart started pounding for a whole new reason. It was Holly, but at this time of day, she should have been in class or in a study group. Was she okay? Lydia had no idea what she would do if she wasn't.

"It's Holly. She almost never calls at this time—I should answer it." Lydia gave Grant an apologetic glance and accepted the call. "Hi, sweetheart. What's up? How are things?"

"Bad," Holly said, sniffling. It did nothing to make her nose sound less stuffed up. "Aiden dumped me."

"Oh, baby, I'm so sorry." Lydia stood, taking a few steps away. "When?"

She turned to Grant, mouthing an apology. He nodded, smiling in understanding. Lydia turned toward the water with her phone still pressed to her ear, soothing her daughter as much as she could. Although her heart was still beating a little harder than usual, and she was very aware of Grant's presence on the bench behind her, she focused on helping her daughter through her first big breakup.

Her own feelings could wait.

CHAPTER FOURTEEN

"Hey, Mom!" Holly called out, rushing from her cab and into Lydia's arms almost before the car had come to a full stop in front of the inn. "It's so good to see you."

"I'm glad you're here, Hols." Lydia squeezed her daughter a little tighter. "Did you have a good trip over?"

"Definitely. I would be happy going literally anywhere off campus. Coming back to Marigold is a treat."

Since Aiden had dumped her a week ago, Holly had told Lydia she didn't want to stick around on campus after the semester ended like she had originally planned to do. The idea of bumping into him was too painful. She had sobbed on the phone for nearly an hour when she'd called, all the way through Lydia and Grant's drive back to the inn, and for good reason.

Lydia fumed just thinking about Aiden. How could anyone dump Holly over a text? He lived in the same dorm on a different floor and he couldn't even tell her to her face?

Lydia took a calming breath. Aiden was in the past now, as she'd told Holly. She would find a guy who would treat her with respect eventually.

At least Holly was going to Spain for a study abroad program in a week, so she could really leave Aiden behind. She wanted to spend at least one week of her summer with Lydia before she left.

"Can I get a tour?" Holly asked, turning to look at the inn. Pride bloomed in Lydia's chest as she watched her daughter take in all the renovations they'd done. It looked fantastic from the outside, much different than the broken-down building it had been just two short months ago.

"Of course!" Lydia grabbed Holly's duffel bag and carried it for her. "The landscaping just got put in last week—the bushes will flower even more before long."

"They're so pretty. And they smell amazing." Holly followed Lydia up the stairs, pointing at a set of rocking chairs near the door. "Ooh, I love these chairs."

"Angela picked them out. They're comfortable, too—we should sit here after dinner." Lydia opened the front door of the inn. "And here's the entryway! I think it's my favorite part."

Holly looked up with an awed expression on her face. All the updates Lydia and Angela had done made walking into the inn a grand experience. It was bright and inviting, the chandelier sparkling where it hung from the ceiling. They'd chosen the perfect shade of blue to compliment the wood of the staircase, a blue that also appeared in the plush rug beneath their feet. Angela had framed some work from local artists, too. They planned to rotate the pieces on display, in collaboration with Nicole's gallery, so that newer artists could get more exposure. Hopefully they could drive traffic to the gallery as well.

"Mom, this is so amazing! And you've done it all so fast." Holly turned in a circle, looking at everything.

Lydia smiled, wrapping an arm around her daughter's shoulders. "Thanks, Hols."

She knew Holly was right. If she put the photos of the inn when they'd bought it next to a picture of what it looked like now, she would hardly have believed the transformation herself. It was exactly like she had hoped it would be—the bones and New England spirit were still there, but they'd brought it into this century.

Lydia gave Holly a tour of the rest of the inn, from the common area, to the dining area, to all the different bedrooms. They ended in the makeshift office area in the back, where Lydia's laptop was sitting. Lydia grabbed them both some iced tea before they sat down.

"And it's so Insta-worthy too," Holly said. She grinned at the question in Lydia's face. "It would look great on Instagram."

"Ah, true. I'd thought of that, but we haven't gotten an account started."

"Can I help? What other social media do you guys have?"

Lydia opened up her laptop and pulled up all the accounts that she and Angela had created. Holly knew exactly what to do, starting an account and pulling in the few photos that Lydia already had on her laptop. Holly was the inn's first follower.

They were so engrossed in working on the marketing that they hardly heard Millie come in through the front door.

"Hello?" Millie called out, her voice echoing through the halls. "Is that Holly I hear?"

Holly hopped up, rushing down the hall like a kid on Christmas morning. Lydia grinned as she watched the two hug for a solid minute, excitedly asking each other how things were going. Holly loved her great-aunt and talked to her on the phone often, but nothing could beat a hug in person.

"Are you two hungry?" Millie asked, her hazel eyes shining.

"I definitely am. Do you want to stay for dinner?" Lydia asked. She had enough ingredients to throw something together.

"Why don't we go out to eat? It's my treat. And we can invite Angela and Jake if they're free," Millie said.

"That sounds perfect!"

Lydia nodded and went to go find Angela, unable to keep the smile off her face. All of her favorite people were finally together. It was going to be a good night.

"I cannot believe how good this cauliflower is," Holly said, covering her mouth so everyone wouldn't see the food inside as she spoke. "How did they make it this good?"

"I swear, roasting any vegetable makes it even better," Angela said, watching as Jake willingly ate some cauliflower too without the tahini sauce. "And it's even better with the chicken."

The restaurant Millie had invited them to had family style dishes. Each of them chose a side dish, though they'd all agreed that they wanted the chicken that was the special of the day as their main dish. Angela had ordered a roasted whole cauliflower with two sauces, a lemon tahini and a pomegranate glaze, and Lydia had picked a fresh salad with nuts and feta cheese. Holly and Millie had gone the more indulgent route with duck fat fries and an assortment of breads and fancy cheeses to dip them in. Jake was going to choose dessert when the time came.

"What else is going on with the inn?" Holly asked Lydia after everyone got over the initial bliss of the delicious food. "Are you settled into the innkeeper's residence all the way?"

"Yep, I'm settled. We're mostly doing the finishing touches on things," Lydia said. "Paint, hardware, little things like that."

Angela nodded. "We're even a little ahead of schedule."

"Do you need any help? I'm completely free for once." Holly laughed. "Well, in between my beach hangouts and naps. I definitely need a lot of naps after staying up so late cramming for finals."

"No, I think we're good. A friend of ours, Grant, is helping," Lydia said. "He's been super helpful with everything. He even saved us from a big leak that would have seriously ruined the innkeeper's house kitchen. His landscaping company was responsible for those bushes you liked."

Angela noticed just how carefully Lydia had said Grant's name, and how much emphasis she put on the words "our friend." Lydia didn't smile, but she didn't frown either, like she was purposefully trying to sound as neutral about Grant as possible.

Since Angela had seen the way the two of them acted around each other, she knew Lydia's tone was an act. They liked each other, clearly, but she wasn't sure whether it was going to turn romantic or not.

But it wasn't her place to pry. If something happened between the two of them, then it was their business, though Angela would be thrilled for her friend if they ended up dating. She wouldn't play matchmaker or bring up anything around Holly, especially since Holly had just gone through a break-up herself.

Holly kept peppering her mom and Millie with questions, trying to get caught up on everything. Even though she was only nineteen, Angela could tell that she worried about her mother just as much as her mother worried about her. It was endearing to see. Angela wondered what it would be like to see Jake go off to college and start his own life. It seemed like he was growing up faster and faster each day.

Angela was interested in the conversation, but still, her eyes couldn't help but wander around the restaurant. She spotted Patrick sitting near the window with his wife. Angela hadn't seen Aubrey since high school, but the woman was still just as pretty as she had been back then. Her long, reddish hair was cut in stylish layers, and her clothes were more reminiscent of something one of Angela's old coworkers back in Philadelphia might wear. People in Marigold were often much more casual, favoring cozy sweaters in the winter or beach t-shirts in the spring and summer.

Patrick leaned forward, putting his hand on Aubrey's. They must have been having a date night.

Angela looked away, not wanting to intrude on a private moment. She focused her attention on the conversation at the table as Jake told a story about a fish he and his grandpa had once caught. She smiled as she watched Millie and Lydia listen with rapt attention.

She still missed Scott sometimes. Missed the easy comfort of family dinners out at restaurants or at home. It was scary to be building a new life for herself and Jake after she'd felt so settled into her life in Philly.

But even though she was starting over, she was starting in a great place.

CHAPTER FIFTEEN

Patrick gave Aubrey's hand another squeeze, almost as if he had to reassure himself that she was really there. They had come to the restaurant for some wine and a few light dishes since Aubrey had eaten a big lunch.

Aubrey had gotten a haircut while she was in Connecticut, and she was wearing an outfit that she hadn't worn in a long time. He wondered what that meant. Aubrey liked to dress up to go out, but he realized that he hadn't seen her do it in a while. Hopefully it was a good sign.

"How's your family?" Patrick asked, sipping his wine. They had spent most of their meal so far in silence, and this was the only thing he could think of saying.

"They're good. Really good." Aubrey spooned some potatoes onto her plate. "They asked about your book—they're all excited for the next one."

"Really? That's great."

Patrick liked her family and always had, even when he was a terrified teenager ringing Aubrey's doorbell to take her on their first date. Over the years since they had been together, her family had supported his writing career and treated him like their own son. It would be so strange to not see them during the holidays if he and Aubrey split up.

"I would ask how the book is going, but, you know." Aubrey gave him a little smile.

They had a long-standing superstition about his work. Almost like flipping a switch, his writing would slow down if she asked him how his manuscript was coming along. It was almost like the "Scottish play" tradition in theater, but Aubrey was the only one who could bring the curse down on him. Saying the words "how is your book going?" would doom Patrick to weeks of bad writing, and there wasn't a cleansing ritual he could do to get rid of it—besides copious amounts of Sweet Creamery ice cream.

Now she just asked how his writing was coming along in a roundabout way, like "how are the crops growing?" or "how's the stock market?" The memory made Patrick smile a little.

They sat in an awkward silence. Usually after a glass of wine, they were able to carry on a normal conversation, but it seemed like neither of them wanted to talk about the one topic they needed to discuss. Aubrey poked at a chunk of potato and ate it, her eyes turning sad.

Finally, she looked up and spoke. "Patrick, I don't want to beat around the bush anymore."

He nodded, feeling his gut start to ache. Any hope that her nice outfit signaled a change of heart flew out the window. He knew what she was going to say.

"We both know I left to get some clarity, and I did. I hope you got some too." Aubrey took a shaky breath. "We tried, Patrick. We really put in the work. And I'm grateful to you for being willing to go see a counselor with me. But it's just... not working. We're too different, and we want different things. I don't feel right asking you to give up on your dream of a family, and I still don't want kids. It's just not in my DNA."

She licked her lips, blinking a little as tears shimmered in her eyes. She squeezed his hand, her expression softening.

"We had some amazing years together, and I'll always be grateful for them. I love you, and I know that's why we lasted as long as we did, despite our differences. But I think, if we stay together, those differences will just become more and more obvious. We'll end up resenting each other, and things will end badly. I'd rather end it while we still care about each other."

Patrick slowly let go of her hand, resting his own in his lap. He'd run this scenario through his head countless times, but actually having it happen felt worse. It felt like someone had literally broken something in his chest, leaving a knot in the base of his throat. He swallowed, pulling himself together.

He was heartbroken. But part of him, deep down, had known this was what Aubrey was going to say. She was right about their differences, and that those difference had become more and more pronounced over the past few years. He loved Aubrey's ambition and didn't want to hold her back from going after what she really wanted.

But still, he hadn't wanted to give up on Aubrey or the idea of their marriage. He loved her, and they'd been together since he was eighteen years old. Now he was thirty-eight. Every single formative event he'd had over the past twenty years had been with her—graduating high school and college, his first job, his first book deal. And he was there for her moments too, both good and bad. People had treated them as a unit—Aubrey and Patrick, Patrick and Aubrey.

And now they wouldn't be that unit anymore.

In some ways, he couldn't imagine what life would look like without her, but he knew he'd have to deal with that reality soon. And he knew she was right that it was better to make this choice now than in another two or five or ten years. If things really weren't working between them, dragging it out would only make it worse.

He had wanted clarity. And now he had it, no matter how much it hurt.

"Okay," was all Patrick was able to say. He took a long sip of wine, trying to get his emotions under control. "I have to admit, I had a feeling this is where things were going. It... it hurts, but I understand. I never want you to hate me or resent me."

Aubrey's eyes glistened. "I still want to be your friend. I can't imagine not being in your life in some way, but I don't think I'm meant to be your wife."

Patrick nodded, studying her face. He could tell this was hurting her as much as it was hurting him. Back in their early twenties when they'd gotten married, he'd imagined their thirties differently. He'd easily thought of them going out to dinners like this, walking along the beach and going home to just cuddle on the couch, maybe even with a dog or a cat.

He'd never thought it would end, though this was probably the best way a divorce could happen—it was amicable enough.

"I want to be your friend too, but I just..." He swallowed, then cleared his throat. "I think I just need a little time before we can do that."

"I understand." She drained the rest of her wine. Both of them still had uneaten food on their plates, but Patrick wasn't sure he could eat another bite. He'd completely lost his appetite. "I'm feeling a little tired, and I should probably give you a little space. I'll sleep in the guest room tonight. I think it's probably best if we both take a bit of space right now."

Patrick could only nod again.

Aubrey stood up, blinking rapidly as she gathered her purse. The familiar scent of her perfume washed over him as she kissed him on the cheek. Then she weaved between the tables in the small restaurant and slipped out the door.

Patrick watched her go, catching her wiping a

tear from her cheek before she disappeared beyond his line of sight.

After a day filled with conversation and laughter, the innkeeper's residence felt extremely quiet that night. Lydia walked as softly as she could to the kitchen to preserve the peace, grabbing a pint of ice cream from The Sweet Creamery and two spoons.

She made her way to the guest room where Holly was staying and knocked softly. Lydia heard her get out of bed to answer. Holly was wearing a big Syracuse t-shirt and pajama pants with cat faces on them, but she looked wide awake.

"Hey, want some?" Lydia held up the ice cream and spoons.

"Always." Holly grinned and stepped back.

Lydia came into the room and sat next to Holly on the bed, holding the ice cream between them. Holly hummed in appreciation. This German chocolate cake flavor had become yet another favorite for Lydia, so she was happy Holly loved it too.

"How are you feeling?" Lydia asked. "Is Marigold a good distraction from Aiden?"

"I think so." Holly spooned up a bite with a chunk of cherry and a chunk of cake. "It really, really hurt at first. It still does, but it's not filling up my life in every single second like it was before."

"That's good."

"Yeah. I think I just fell too hard, too fast." Holly shrugged. "But at least I know that now. Getting way too attached, way too fast isn't a good idea."

Lydia nodded. She was glad she hadn't told Holly about the risks of falling in love fast before this happened. She hated to see her daughter upset, but she also knew that Holly could have a stubborn streak sometimes—if Lydia had pressed the issue, Holly might not have learned this important part of herself.

"And anyway, it's summer, and I deserve to have fun in Spain instead of worrying about some guy. My friend Jenna—you remember Jenna, right? Well, she's studying abroad in France, and we're going to visit each other, so I'll get to see even more of Europe. We might even take a weekend trip to Germany or England."

Lydia smiled. She admired how adventurous Holly was. She didn't let her fears hold her back from trying new things. She was like her father in that way.

"I'm so excited for you, sweetheart. I know you'll have a great time, even though I know I'm going to be worried sick if you don't call me."

"Of course. If you weren't worried, I'd think you were body-snatched by aliens."

Both of them laughed, resting their spoons inside the now-empty pint. Lydia leaned over to put it on the side table so it was out of the way. When she turned back to Holly, her daughter's smile had faded.

"What's wrong? Are you worried too?" Lydia asked. "It'll be your first time travelling abroad alone."

"No, not worried." Holly leaned back into the pillows, curling her knees up to her chest. "I just want you to be happy. Not that you seem *unhappy*, and it seems like Marigold is good for you. I just hope that it stays that way."

"It is really good for me." Lydia mirrored Holly's position. "I feel more alive here than I have in a long time. I don't want to leave."

"Well, good. I think you'd be miserable going back to Boston." Holly wrinkled her nose. "Plus, it's so much nicer here and the food is amazing."

"I'd be lying if I said the food wasn't a big part of the attraction." Lydia rested a hand on her stomach, which felt content and filled with ice cream. "But there are so many things I love about this place. Marigold has become *home* so fast. Everyone's become like family already."

Was Grant part of the reason why it had become home, too? She'd gotten used to him dropping by all the time, helping her reach things that were too high and keeping her company even during the most mundane tasks. Their conversations felt easy, and she could count on feeling better after. He was gruff, sure, and not the perkiest person, but he still lightened up her days regardless.

Lydia blinked, pulling herself out of her thoughts. She and Holly had literally just discussed falling in love too fast, and here she was, at risk of doing just that.

But she couldn't deny that her feelings for Grant were progressing beyond simple friendship.

CHAPTER SIXTEEN

Between Holly being in town and working to get the inn ready for its rapidly approaching opening day, Angela's life was hectic. A fun hectic, but hectic nonetheless.

Angela and Lydia showed Holly around the island, which reacquainted Holly with parts of Marigold she'd forgotten. Lydia and Paul had brought her to the small town as often as they could when Holly was growing up, but she hadn't been back in years. Just as Angela and Lydia had been when they'd first come back, Holly was pleasantly surprised at all the cool new things Marigold had to offer.

One of those things was the newer tradition of summer parades. People would gather around Main

Street for fun, and businesses along the street would hold special events or hand out food or gifts just for the occasion. Holly didn't want to miss it, and neither did Jake, so Angela found herself tucked into a cluster of people along Main Street, watching the nearby high school's band camp march along with their instruments.

Other friends and family had come with them too—Angela's parents, Brooke, Lydia, Millie, and Grant. Travis was the only one missing, and that was because he was on duty, working with a few other police officers to make sure the parade was safe and well-run. Angela spotted him for a moment, guiding a cluster of people across the parade route, and waved.

After they watched for a while, Angela took Jake to the restroom in one of the shops. On their way out, they bumped into Patrick, who was lingering toward the back of the crowd alongside the parade route.

"You always seem to catch me when I'm skipping out on writing," Patrick said with a smile.

"I do?" Angela smiled back, keeping an eye on Jake so he didn't go running off into the crowd. A shop owner a door down gave him a bubble solution and a wand, which he quickly fell in love with. He ran the wand through the air and popped the bubbles one by one.

"Yeah." Patrick tucked his hands into his pockets. "But it's kind of part of my process. Sometimes I have to let things sit because forcing it doesn't get me anywhere. They just have to come to me."

"Creativity's tricky like that."

"True. I feel like I wander around town, eating ice cream and buying more books that I don't need all the time." Patrick shrugged.

"So even writers end up with a to-read stack that's as tall as they are?"

"Oh, we're the worst. I have an entire shelf of books that I haven't gotten to yet. I always jump to the shiniest book in the pile, then end up adding even more. Plus my publisher sends me books from other authors that he thinks I'll like," Patrick said. "I always get distracted when I'm stuck in moments like this."

"I bet."

Patrick deflated a little. "Some days, I worry that the ideas will never show up again. I see all these other writers churning out books faster than I could ever dream and panic a little."

"I'm sure they will! Some of the greatest authors

only put out a few books. And you're a great writer, Patrick."

"You think so?" He looked genuinely surprised at the compliment.

"Yeah. I've read a few of your books and really loved them." Angela noticed his cheeks flush a little and found it strangely endearing. "And I'm not just saying that."

"Thank you."

As they spoke, Angela wandered a little farther into the crowd behind Jake, and Patrick followed. A refurbished classic car went down the route in front of them, and Jake had to run to keep up with it. He didn't have to know a lot about the vehicles in order to appreciate them, and he'd loved cars for as long as Angela could remember.

Unfortunately, he was paying a bit too much attention to the car and not enough to where he was running. He tripped on a loose bit of cement, toppling down to the ground and catching himself so he didn't fall flat on his face—his wrist took the impact instead.

He burst into tears right away, and Angela's heart lurched in her chest. She pushed through the crowd, not caring if she was being rude. Jake was injured, and that was her sole focus at that moment.

She kneeled down beside him as people gave them space. No one could hear him crying over the noise of the parade.

"It hurts," Jake sobbed.

"I know, sweetheart." Angela stroked his hair and pressed his head to her chest.

The parade wasn't going to stop for one little boy. How were they going to get to the doctor with all the roads closed to accommodate the parade's path? She'd come to know the island pretty well in her time there, but not well enough to get to the doctor quickly if she had to modify her route. Panic rose in her chest, but she stayed steady. Jake would freak out even more if she showed her nerves.

"Do you want a ride? My car's not far, and I know a way around all this traffic," Patrick said, crouching down next to them.

"Could you really? We would appreciate it so much."

"It's the least I can do. Follow me."

Angela slipped into the crowd to tell her family and friends where they were going, then helped Jake to Patrick's car. They got Jake tucked into the back seat and zoomed as fast as they could toward the doctor's office.

* * *

Patrick glanced at Jake in the rearview mirror. The little boy was still sniffling and cradling his swollen wrist. Angela kept turning to look back at her son with worried glances. Patrick totally understood her fears, and he remembered breaking his own wrist as a kid—the painful snap, the inexplicable nausea, the fear. Jake needed a distraction. No one liked going to the doctor's office, but kids really, really hated it.

"Hey, do you want to hear a joke?" Patrick asked Jake.

"Okay." Jake wiped his eyes.

"What do you give a sick lemon?"

"I dunno."

"Lemon-aid."

Patrick had to grin even though the joke was cheesy, but it had its intended effect—Jake laughed a little. He saw Angela shoot him a small smile out of the corner of his eye, one that was both a little grateful and a bit amused.

The drive was much longer because of the parade, so Patrick tried to fill it all to keep Jake's mind off his pain. He ran through all the kid-friendly jokes he had, then switched to all the trivia that a kid might know or be interested in. Jake knew a surprising amount about animals, so Patrick had to dig deep to think of something that would blow his mind.

"Did you know that there's only one mammal in the whole world that's covered in scales, kind of like a fish?" Patrick asked, pulling into the parking lot of the hospital. "It's called a pangolin. Their tongues are longer than their whole bodies."

"Wow... how does that work? Where does it go? Are their mouths really big?" Jake asked, now wide-eyed in wonder despite the fact that his wrist had swollen even more.

"We can look it up when we get inside," Angela said, unbuckling her seatbelt. "Let's go get your wrist looked at."

They all went in, and thankfully, the wait was short. They sat down in the waiting room, showing Jake pictures of pangolins on Angela's phone to pass the time. It really was an odd-looking creature, but Jake found it cute. He couldn't believe its tongue could fit into its body.

Soon, a nurse came to take Jake to get his wrist x-rayed. Angela and Patrick followed them, although they couldn't go into the room where the x-ray was being taken. There was yet another waiting area for them to sit in a few feet away. Angela fidgeted with her watch, keeping her eyes on the door to the x-ray room.

"You don't have to stay. You've already done so much," she told Patrick once Jake was settled in the x-ray room. "You're missing the rest of the parade."

"It's fine. I've seen it before. And it's probably over by now, I bet. I really don't mind keeping you company."

Angela nodded, smiling wider than she had since she'd seen Jake go down on the asphalt. Patrick really didn't mind—he was happy to help her. And Jake.

After several minutes, the little boy came out with his arm in a temporary sling and sat in the waiting room with them so the doctor could look at his x-rays and figure out what to do next. Even though the wait wasn't long, it was still getting late in the afternoon. Patrick hadn't grabbed any of the special treats being offered by the restaurants along the parade route, so he was getting hungry. They'd passed a vending machine, though. Maybe he would see if Angela or Jake wanted anything to snack on.

But before he could ask them if they wanted anything from the machine, Angela stiffened in surprise. Patrick followed her gaze down the hallway and caught sight of a worried looking man dressed in a polo shirt and shorts.

"Jake, buddy!" The man said.

Jake's face lit up, and he carefully walked closer to the man, as if worried that he'd trip and fall again in the flat hallway.

The man gingerly wrapped his arms around Jake, who squeezed him with his good arm. Then the man hugged Angela, who still appeared to be in a state of mild shock.

"Scott, wow. What are you doing here?" she asked, stepping back.

Patrick quickly put the pieces together by looking at all three of them together. Jake looked just like both of them, and he remembered Angela saying that she had come to Marigold after splitting up with her husband.

There was no question about it—her ex had arrived.

CHAPTER SEVENTEEN

Angela was too shocked to turn down Scott's hug, but eventually, she snapped out of it and stepped out of his grasp. She looked him up and down. He looked about the same as he had when she'd seen him last, although he'd grown back his beard.

"What are you doing here?" she asked again.

"I came to visit, like I mentioned I wanted to last time we spoke on the phone. I wanted to support you and Lydia with the inn and to see how it's coming along." Scott shrugged. "I stopped by the parade when I arrived on Marigold. Lydia told me what happened, so I rushed over."

Angela nodded slowly, trying to readjust into a calm state again. She hadn't expected to see her estranged husband today, and she was having a hard time regaining her equilibrium. Luckily, Scott sat down and talked to Jake about what happened, comforting him and telling him how brave he was. Jake got so distracted that he started talking about the parade again, filling his dad in on all the cool stuff he'd seen before the fall. Scott was completely focused on his son.

"Hey, it looks like things are under control. I'm going to head out," Patrick said, putting his hand on her shoulder.

"Oh, okay." Angela blinked, clearing her vision. "Thank you so much again. It really means a lot."

She wasn't sure what else she could possibly say to express her gratitude. She wanted to see Patrick again, maybe take him to lunch as another thank you for helping to steady everyone's nerves. His jokes were corny, but Jake had loved them, and she was honestly impressed with all the animal trivia he knew.

But would going out to lunch with him even be appropriate? Patrick was married—she had just seen him with Aubrey the other day. And technically, Angela was too, since their divorce hadn't been finalized yet. Just because Scott had been unfaithful didn't mean she felt okay with skirting the line of what was and wasn't right.

"You're welcome," Patrick said. "See you around."

He said goodbye to Jake and Scott and headed down the hall, leaving Angela with her almost ex-husband and son. It was a little surreal seeing Scott in the place that she'd turned into her new home, but the familiarity of seeing him joking around with Jake made things feel a bit less strained.

Angela gently rubbed at her chest, as if that could soothe the confused ache she felt. In spite of his failings as a husband, Scott was a good dad. He loved Jake fiercely, just as much as Jake loved him. Scott had been there for Jake every step of the way as he grew up, for every sick day and every soccer game, without a single complaint. She couldn't have asked for anything more on that front.

Should I try again with Scott, for Jake's sake? Angela wondered. *Maybe it would be better for him to have both of his parents together...*

She turned the question around in her head over and over again while Jake got his break set and a cast put on. Once the doctor gave the okay, they walked out. Since Scott had a car, they hitched a ride with him back to the inn. Jake quickly fell asleep in the back seat, as he often did on car rides.

"I want to give our marriage a second shot,

Angie." Scott kept his voice low enough for Jake to not wake up. They'd perfected whispered conversations, since Jake had been a light sleeper when he was a baby.

"Scott..."

As Angela's voice trailed off, he pulled up to the inn and put the car in park. She fiddled with her watch, unsure of what to say. It felt like the hundredth time he'd asked, but this time, the words got through to her. Seeing Scott and Jake together had broken down some of the defenses she'd built around her heart. She wanted to do what was best for her, but she had to consider what would be best for her son, too.

"Please?"

"I'll think about it," she said after a long pause. "Let's get Jake inside."

Lydia's mouth watered as heavenly aromas filled the air. The kitchen in the inn had never smelled this good.

She, Millie, Angela, Holly, and Jake were all crowded into the small space, watching Brooke pull her first batch of cinnamon scones out of the oven.

She put them next to the lemon poppyseed muffins that she'd already finished. They were test runs for the pastries she hoped to serve to guests.

"Does anyone want some fresh coffee?" Lydia asked, holding up the pot.

"I'd love some," Millie said, eyeing the muffins. "Can we dig into the muffins yet, Brooke?"

"Yep! They should be cool enough." Brooke took a step back as everyone grabbed a muffin.

Lydia moaned softly as she took her first bite. They were perfect on their own, but they were even better with coffee. The muffin managed to be a real muffin, not just a cupcake that had lost its icing. It was light and fluffy, with the sharp lemon zest balanced out by just the right amount of sweetness. Guests would love them.

After everyone got a good fill of the muffins, Holly took Jake into the next room to play a board game while the other adults waited for the scones to cool, staring at them as if they could cool them down faster. Lydia glanced through the door at Holly, who was laughing just as hard as Jake was at the goofy game they'd unearthed from the inn's basement. They'd bonded in the short time that Holly had been on Marigold, almost like long-lost siblings, and Lydia was happy to see it.

"Scott is in town," Angela said after a brief lull in conversation. There was a heaviness to her voice, and she spoke quickly, as if she needed to get the words out.

Lydia frowned, even though she was the one who'd pointed him in the direction of the doctor's office. She wasn't a fan of him, to put it lightly, but he'd deserved to see his injured child.

"Really? Since when?" Brooke asked.

"Since yesterday. He drove us back from the hospital." Angela absently swirled her coffee around in her mug. "He said he wanted to try to patch things up, and coming here is a pretty big step. He's staying at the South Cove B&B across town for a while."

"Do you want to give him another shot?" Millie asked, brushing a strand of dark gray hair back from her face.

Angela looked at the ceiling, searching for her words. "I don't know if I want to be married to him anymore, but I can't make the decision based only on what I feel. There's Jake. I want to do what's best for him."

Brooke gently rubbed her sister's shoulders as everyone else murmured in understanding. It was a hard place to be. Lydia knew Angela was loyal to a fault and loved her son more than anything in the world. But being cheated on, maybe repeatedly, was no way to live. Still, Lydia couldn't tell her friend what to do in a situation like this—she could only be someone to lean on.

"We'll be here for you," she promised. "No matter what happens."

"Thanks, guys." Angela managed to smile a little, finishing off her muffin. "Sorry to bring the mood down."

"Don't apologize. This is what friends are for. And we're already eating a bunch of sugar—it's the perfect place to air things out," Millie said, making everyone laugh.

"I think the scones should be cool enough to taste now," Brooke said, touching a scone with the backs of her fingers.

She didn't have to tell anyone twice. They all inhaled the scones, which were just as delicious as the muffins. The bits of cinnamon had the tiniest kick to them, and chasing them with coffee made the flavors meld together beautifully. They were perfect for a light but indulgent breakfast.

"This scone is unreal," Lydia said through a mouthful. "This test run has been the best idea any of us have had in a long time."

The other women agreed, finding the extra room

in their stomachs they needed to eat more scones. The mood lifted slightly until Angela got a text. Her smile rapidly fell flat as she read it, her brows furrowed.

Was it Scott? How else could he disappoint or upset her?

"What is it?" Lydia asked, unsure of what answer was waiting. "Is everything okay?"

CHAPTER EIGHTEEN

"It's from Jennifer from the real estate office," Angela said, swallowing the lump that had appeared in her throat. "There's a problem. Her text says, *just wanted to give you a heads up—it looks like Hunter Reed bought a lot of property on the waterfront. He wants to try to build a big hotel on it.*"

The room was silent, though everyone's faces lit up with shock.

"*The* Hunter Reed? The famous actor? That Hunter Reed?" Brooke finally asked, her eyebrows so high that they nearly disappeared into her hairline.

"I'm guessing yes. I don't know any other Hunter Reeds." Angela stared at her phone. "Of all the places in the world, I never thought a movie star would buy land in Marigold. It's really far from Hollywood."

"I don't know if he's acting as much anymore." Brooke shrugged. "The last big movie he was in came out a couple years ago, I think."

"Maybe he's just diversifying or trying to make a career shift?" Lydia pursed her lips. "He's, what, in his thirties now? He was really popular back in his early twenties, doing all those summer blockbusters and stuff. He probably doesn't want to do roles like that anymore."

Angela vaguely remembered seeing him in movies, although most of the ones he'd starred in weren't exactly her preferred genre. She'd seen him more often in commercials or on TV shows promoting his work. He seemed nice enough, but that didn't mean anything in the world of business. He was an actor, and he could look any way he wanted to on TV.

"His career situation is secondary to the big hotel part," she said, shaking her head as she re-read the text on her phone. "If he opens a big hotel with fancy amenities, we won't have a chance. We already have competition from the other inns and B&Bs on the island."

"Did Jennifer clarify what she meant by big

hotel? There's 'big hotel' in the city sense, then big for Marigold," Millie said.

Angela shot Jennifer another text, which the real estate agent responded to right away. Angela felt like her lungs were slowly constricting.

"He's thinking like hotel chain big," Angela said. "He has potential investors and everything. Imagine a Hilton or a Sheraton, right in the middle of the boardwalk. That's what Hunter wants."

The room went quiet again, somberness settling over them as everyone absorbed what that meant. With a big hotel nearby, no one would get the chance to see all the work they'd done or experience all the memories that they hoped their guests would make. They knew that people would come to Marigold specifically for the New England inn experience, but an equal number of people would be attracted to what was familiar—neutral, uniform hotel rooms with fancy room service and cable.

All their work would be for nothing.

Holly came back into the kitchen with Jake, catching her mother's gaze with a worried look. Angela stuffed down her fears, or at least made sure they weren't too evident, and grabbed a scone for Jake. He tasted it, nodding and smiling in approval.

Jake was a smart boy, but Angela hoped he wouldn't pick up on her mood.

"I overheard what's going on," Holly said. "That sucks. I like Hunter Reed's movies, but I hate that his plans might mess things up for you guys. He's a good actor—not that he ever gets to do much serious acting in those big budget blockbusters."

"Well, those blockbusters have made him enough money to open a big fancy hotel, apparently," Lydia said, sounding dejected as her face fell. Angela had never seen her look that way, and it broke her heart.

Holly gave her mom a hug. "It'll be okay. You guys have already done all this work, and you have so much more passion for Marigold than practically anyone. You can find a way."

"Yeah," Brooke said, her face lighting up as she quickly jumped on the optimism Holly was offering. "If anyone can make this work, it's you two."

Angela's eyes got misty as she looked at all of her friends around her. She locked gazes with Lydia and nodded. This wasn't the end.

They could figure out a way to move forward.

* * *

By the time lunch rolled around, Lydia hadn't gotten over her fears about the future of the inn. Jennifer had agreed to meet her and Angela for lunch to give them the scoop. Lydia hoped things would look better with a little more information, but she still wasn't hopeful. This new hotel was like a sudden slap in the face. Once they'd bought the inn, she'd thought their only problems would be from within, but here was this brand new challenge.

They settled on one of the many seafood places on the waterfront, not too far from the property that Hunter Reed had purchased. They met Jennifer outside the restaurant, Glenn's Crab Shack, then headed inside together and were seated by the hostess. When the waiter came to take their orders, Lydia decided to treat herself to a lobster roll, and the others chose the catch of the day. All of it was incredibly fresh and flavorful, which brightened Lydia's mood a bit.

"So, my colleague who handled Hunter's deal told me more about his plans for the land. He wants to rezone it into commercial land and build a hotel there since it's a great spot and tourism is really picking up. It'll be like a Hilton or something along those lines, like I said." Jennifer must have noticed

Lydia's expression fall, because she added, "But don't give up hope."

"What can we do?" Lydia asked, putting down her lobster roll.

"You could try talking to Hunter, which might work. I haven't met him, but my colleague said he was friendly enough." Jennifer shrugged.

"Do you really think he'd listen? We're just two random women he's never met," Angela said. "And we're his competition. I don't think he'd care about our feelings on the matter."

"True. But it would be better to try than to not, right?" Lydia swirled her straw in her drink. "Even if it's a total long shot."

"Yeah." Angela heaved a sigh.

"The more feasible option would probably be to voice objections at the rezoning hearing," Jennifer said. "That way, you could get other people in town on your side to object to the rezoning too. If they make a good case for why it wouldn't be good for the community, the property might not be rezoned."

Lydia took that in, taking another bite of her roll. That might work. She had been to a rezoning meeting back in Boston when some company tried to turn old houses into a mega-store that would have killed the neighborhood's charm and made traffic horrific. It had worked—they'd been able to keep the company out, and private buyers had bought the old houses to flip.

And that was in the big city. Marigold was so much more tight-knit.

"That sounds like it could work," Lydia said.

"Yeah. And I'm sure Millie knows a bunch of people to reach out to. People who are really passionate about Marigold's future." Angela sounded hopeful again.

"Exactly! Everyone knows Millie," Lydia said with a laugh. "Marigold residents seem really passionate about the island, and they live here for a reason. It's a special place, so I bet we could drum up the support we need."

The women discussed how they might go about gathering members of the community to object to the rezoning, bouncing ideas off of each other and thinking up people to reach out to. By the end of lunch, Lydia finally felt like they had a firm grip on the inn's future again. They could do this. It would take a lot of enthusiasm and determination, but luckily, they had plenty of both.

"We really can't thank you enough. You didn't have to help us like this," Angela said, shaking Jennifer's hand outside of the restaurant.

"It's really no problem." The chestnut-haired woman grinned. "I'm so happy you two ended up getting the inn, and I'd love to see it thrive."

"I'm surprised we got it at all. We weren't sure if we could beat Grant's offer." Lydia shook Jennifer's hand too before reaching into her purse for her car keys. "We were terrified we'd end up in a bidding war."

Jennifer cocked her head to the side, her pretty features scrunching in confusion. "Oh. Grant withdrew his bid. Did he not tell you?

"Wait, really?" Lydia stopped digging through her purse. She knew she would remember if he'd told her that—he definitely hadn't.

"Yeah, he did."

"When?"

"Right after the open house. I don't know what could have possibly changed his mind, but he came up to me and said he was bowing out." Jennifer shrugged. "Either way, you two got it and deserve it, especially with all the hard work you've put in."

Lydia couldn't believe it. A pleasant warmth filled her chest as she contemplated Jennifer's words. Had Grant withdrawn his bid for her? She knew that the inn looked like a good investment on the inside, so she doubted he had seen anything to turn him off from it. Or did he just decide not to bid for some other reason?

The Grant she knew didn't do things without a good reason, but Lydia couldn't be sure. It might have been a big coincidence.

CHAPTER NINETEEN

Lydia didn't want Holly to leave Marigold, but she had to let her go. The week of Holly's visit had gone by faster than Lydia would've thought possible. She hopped out of the car when they arrived at the ferry and hugged her daughter so tightly that Holly groaned in mock protest.

"Promise me you'll be safe. But have fun and be smart too, okay?" Lydia went back in for another short hug.

"I will. And you do the same, all right? Promise?"

"I promise."

"I know you'll be able to deal with the hotel, too." Holly hiked her duffel bag higher on her shoulder. "I'm really excited to come back and see the

Beachside Inn in the fall, especially when all the leaves start changing and all the guests arrive."

"I'm excited too. Love you. Call me when you get to the airport. And when you're about to take off. And—"

"—and when I land. I know." Holly kissed Lydia on the cheek. "Love you lots, Mom."

Holly ran to the ferry and boarded just before it pulled away. She waved to Lydia once she got to the deck, and Lydia watched the boat pull away. Wiping a few happy tears from her eyes, she hopped back into her car and drove toward the inn.

She hoped Holly would have a good time abroad and *really* hoped that she could keep a lid on all of her worries. She never wanted to discourage Holly or make her worry about her own mother. Holly was responsible and had a good head on her shoulders. Things would be okay.

Lydia took a deep breath to steady herself, remembering what Holly had told her—that she wanted Lydia to stay happy. She couldn't stay happy if she spent all day and night worrying about whether Holly was homesick or if her Spanish was good enough for her to get around.

Lydia sped up when she realized she was at risk of running late. She needed to shift her attention to the other big thing in her life—the inn. If she, Angela, and Brooke couldn't pull off their plan, Holly wouldn't get to see it in its full glory in the fall. They had outlined a plan to deal with Hunter's proposed hotel, starting with the smallest step first. They were going to pay the actor a visit, bearing Brooke's amazing pastries as a peace offering. Hopefully, they could have a productive and civil conversation with him.

When Lydia reached the inn, Brooke and Angela were waiting for her, an adorable wicker basket of baked goods sitting between them on the front porch.

"Ready to start phase one of our plan?" Brooke asked, standing.

"Let's do it."

Angela pulled her hair back into a ponytail so she wouldn't nervously play with it as she had on the entire drive over to Hunter's house. It was situated on the waterfront, one of the larger, nicer homes that had popped up on the island in recent years. The walk up to the front door was a little intimidating. The house wasn't the fanciest on the island, but it was definitely up there, large and luxurious with a sleek, modern design.

Angela raised her hand to press the doorbell, but hesitated. They still had time to turn back. This was going to be a disaster.

"I've got it." Brooke leaned past her and poked the doorbell, then stepped back with her basket on her arm.

Angela was always much more worried than Brooke was, but for once, she felt like her fears were totally justified. This was a crazy plan. They couldn't show up to a world-famous actor's house with some baked goods and hope to change his mind. But it was too late to turn back—the door opened.

It was strange seeing Hunter Reed's face in person after seeing him on her TV and at the movies for so long. He was even more handsome in person. Angela hadn't even thought that was possible. His dark brown hair was perfectly messy, and the dark gray eyes that had audiences swooning were even more beautiful up close. He hardly had to say a word to charm them.

He smiled, though he looked confused. All of them, even Brooke, were just staring at him in mild shock or anxiety or both.

"Um, hey!" Brooke finally said, extending the

basket filled with treats. "We just wanted to welcome you to the island with some freshly baked pastries. Just to say hello."

"Oh, that's really nice of you all. Come on in." He stepped back and let them into his home.

It was beautifully designed, filled with pieces and brands that Angela had only been able to buy for the wealthiest clients she had back in Philadelphia.

The house had been renovated to open up the entryway, allowing even more light to spill into the space. Hunter took them all the way to the back living room, which had more than enough space for all of them. The entire back wall had been replaced with floor to ceiling windows, making the ocean almost like an extra piece of art.

"I'm Hunter Reed," he said, gesturing for them to sit. Then he gave a charming, self-deprecating grin. "Although you may have already known that. And what are your names?"

"I'm Brooke, and this is my older sister Angela and her friend Lydia." Brooke put the basket of goodies on the marble table in between all the seats.

"Nice to meet all of you." He sounded genuinely happy. "Would you ladies like something to drink? Coffee? Tea?"

"Coffee would be great if it's not too much trouble," Brooke said.

Angela almost laughed. It felt like Brooke was the only one who could speak. Angela herself was still a little stunned that Hunter had let them in, and he still looked a little confused as to why they were there. He left the living room, and after a few short moments, he came back with a stainless steel pot filled with coffee, some mugs, and some small plates. He poured them each a drink before settling onto a finely upholstered chair.

Angela didn't know much about coffee, aside from the fact that she needed the boost of caffeine every morning and enjoyed her morning ritual, but she could tell this coffee was high end. She could almost taste the notes that the inexpensive bags of coffee she got at the grocery store claimed they had—cherry, chocolate, and vanilla. It went down smoothly, even without milk or cream.

"This is delicious, thank you," she said.

"You're welcome." He smiled and put a cinnamon scone on his plate. "What brings you all here, besides the warm welcome?"

"We own the inn down the street," Lydia said, grabbing her own pastry.

"Ah, yeah, I saw it. It looks great. My real estate

agent said that it was being renovated." He broke off a piece of scone. "You two are doing that?"

"Yeah, we are. We did a lot of the work ourselves." Angela took a scone too and hoped she didn't look like she was stress eating. "We're finishing up the final touches."

"Wow, that's awesome." He nodded and popped the scone into his mouth. His face lit up as he chewed, an expression Angela had gotten familiar with when watching anyone try Brooke's baked goods. "Where did you get these scones? They're incredible."

"Oh, I made them." Brooke raised her hand a little, her cheeks going bright pink.

His eyebrows shot up appreciatively. "They're seriously good. They're better than most of the pastries I've had in New York City or LA, by a long shot." He broke off another chunk and ate it. "But, yeah, so you guys own the inn? I guess that means we'll be competitors then, when I get my hotel up and running."

Angela looked at Lydia, who nodded.

"That's part of why we came here," Angela said carefully. "We both adore Marigold—my entire family lives here, and Lydia has so many amazing memories of coming here during the summer. Part of what makes us love it here is its small town charm with all the local businesses and the slower pace. We're concerned that opening a huge hotel here will take away everything that makes Marigold the place it is."

Angela let out a shaky breath. She'd said what they rehearsed in the car, but now that she was actually saying it, she was terrified they'd made a mistake. Hunter sat back in his seat, crossing one ankle over his knee, and studied them.

"Hm, okay," he said slowly, sipping his coffee.

"Would you reconsider your plan to get the land rezoned for the hotel?" Lydia asked. "We're not just asking because we also own the inn. We would reach out to any business that wouldn't be the best for Marigold in the long run."

Hunter seemed to turn the thought of it over in his head. The delicious coffee started to turn bitter in Angela's mouth.

"I can see that. You all are clearly nice people, and you care about the island. The thing is that I disagree. A hotel could be exactly what Marigold needs." Hunter put his cup down and sat back again.

"How so?" Brooke asked, her brows furrowing.

"Well, more people could come to the island in general because there would be more places for people to stay. People are more likely to come if they know they can find a good place to stay at a moment's notice. And it's right on the beach, which many smaller places—your inn excluded—aren't. The hotel could also create a lot of good jobs for the island too." He ticked off each of his points with his well-manicured fingers.

Angela watched Lydia deflate a little. He did have some good points. Their inn would provide a few jobs, but not nearly as many as a big hotel would. In the end, people would want Marigold to prosper and for more people to find steady work. And there weren't a lot of places for people to stay along the beach, which was one of the biggest reasons why people came to town anyway. The views from other inns on the island were nice, but nothing could beat the view of the water.

Angela picked up another scone and broke into it, trying to keep her hands busy as Hunter continued.

"Plus, some people want just a little taste of small town while they're out and about. They might want to come back to a comfortable hotel room with cable and a gym." He shrugged, as if he'd already polled all of his future guests about what they wanted out of their trip to Marigold.

Angela bit her bottom lip and looked to Lydia, but it was Brooke who spoke.

"You have a point," she said carefully. "But that still doesn't mean it won't change the feeling of the island. That's a big reason why so many people have lived here for decades, and this new hotel with all the amenities people can get anywhere else would change the vibe of the community. I mean, I've lived here all my life because I know the stuff the bigger cities have isn't nearly as special as what's here."

"Exactly. I lived in Philadelphia up until recently, and as much as our real estate agent talked about our particular neighborhood being a true community, it doesn't have anything on Marigold." Angela hoped the passion in her voice didn't come across as confrontational, but she really believed in what she was saying. "Making the town more typically touristy could create that 'tourist versus local' dynamic that a lot of cities have. Right now, people welcome tourists with open arms, but all of that could change if the balance tips just a little."

"I get all of that, I really do." Hunter smiled, almost as if to soothe them. He really was frustratingly charming, and his obvious sincerity only made it harder to dislike him. "I should probably add that I really care about the island too.

I'm not just some Hollywood type trying to bring a piece of the big city here, I promise. I want to be here specifically because it's the opposite of LA. That's not the life for me anymore, and it would be pretty silly for me to permanently change the community that I want to be a part of."

He sounded genuine. Holly had mentioned that his last big movie was a couple years ago, and he really did seem like he wanted to settle down a bit. Marigold was just the right place for people who wanted to slow down and have true neighbors instead of strangers who lived next door.

"The hotel would have a lot of the same New England beach town charm in its style, too," he added. "I grew up in a little town like this and have always loved the architecture and design. I've been talking to some designers who have worked on my homes before and they think they can blend the old with newer features that a lot of people look for when they're splurging on a trip."

Angela believed in her abilities as an interior designer, especially after all the work they'd done in the inn, but she knew that their limited budget hadn't allowed her to do everything she wanted. If the hotel looked anything like his home, people who were attracted to higher-end places would likely choose Hunter's hotel over the inn. The inn's bathrooms were nice, but they weren't the kind with massive clawfoot tubs or heated floors. They definitely didn't have a gym or anything like that either.

But that wasn't what the inn was about, anyway.

Hunter took another scone, downing it in a few short bites. The women stayed quiet, absorbing everything he'd said. Even though Angela knew that every point he'd made was valid—even though he seemed extremely confident that the hotel would open according to plan—she also knew that their points were just as valid.

"I can tell you've put a lot of thought into this," Lydia said, folding her hands in her lap. "But I don't think we can just back down on this. Do you guys agree?"

Angela and Brooke nodded. Hunter was extremely charming, but she knew deep down that a big hotel wasn't what the island needed. This was about more than just keeping the Beachside Inn from having to compete with a larger business. It was about preserving what was special about the place she'd come to call home.

"I understand." Hunter smiled, brushing scone crumbs off his fingers and onto the plate. He glanced inside the basket, his smile dimming a little when he realized they'd eaten everything. Then he glanced up, meeting each of their gazes. "Tell you what—I don't want there to be any bad blood between us, so can we agree to let the zoning board decide? If they deny my request to rezone, I'll drop the idea. I won't appeal the decision or make any other plans to develop that stretch of oceanside property."

"Really?" Angela's eyebrows shot up.

Hunter's gray eyes were sincere. "Sure. But if they approve it, I'll go ahead with my plans for development. Sound fair?"

Lydia nodded slowly, worry filling her features as she glanced at Angela. Then determination replaced the concern. "Okay," she said. "If you're willing to stand by the zoning board's decision, we are too. But we'll definitely plan on making our case to them."

"Of course. As will I." Hunter gave a lopsided shrug, a dimple appearing as his cheek as he grinned again. "And whatever happens, happens."

CHAPTER TWENTY

"You're sure you've got a good hold on the ladder?" Lydia asked Grant, looking down at him from her spot above him. "It's really old and feels a little wobbly from here."

Grant looked up at her, a dark eyebrow going up. Lydia knew that the eyebrow was Grant's way of saying *seriously?* She'd come to learn his secret expression language over the past couple months. He might not have been the most outwardly expressive man she'd ever met, but his little mouth quirks, brow furrows, and eyebrow movements said a lot if you paid enough attention.

"I've got it, Lydia. You're about three feet off the ground." He steadied his grip on the ladder anyway. "You're more at risk of knocking yourself out with that curtain rod than hurting yourself from a fall."

Lydia looked back down at the curtain rod she was about to place. He was right—the rods that Angela had picked out were surprisingly heavy and looked great. She would be in trouble if she let it fall on her head. That gave Lydia a little extra incentive to put up the curtain rods well; they couldn't have guests getting hurt because of a mistake she'd made.

Lydia screwed in the piece that held the rod on each side of the window and put the rod into place. Grant helped her down, and they moved their ladder and tools into the next room, where they had to hang the next set. Grant took the lead this time, getting up on the ladder with the necessary tools.

Lydia gripped the shakier parts of the old ladder, which they'd found when they went back through the basement. The bedroom they were in had a view of the water, much like many of the rooms Hunter's hotel would have if the zoning board decided in his favor.

"You all right?" Grant asked.

"Hm? Oh, yeah. I'm just thinking about the hotel that Hunter Reed wants to open. I went with Angela and Brooke—and some of Brooke's amazing scones— to welcome him and hopefully get him to rethink his plans." Lydia sighed and resisted the urge to rest her head against the ladder.

"Was he charmed by those scones? If someone came to my house with those, they could sell me on anything." Grant turned a screw one more time and gestured for the rod.

"He was charmed. He even said that they were better than scones he'd had in New York and LA," Lydia said, a small smile returning to her face.

The ride back to the inn had been quiet except for when they'd talked about how cool it was that someone who had travelled all over and eaten at the best places in the world loved Brooke's scones. Brooke was thrilled.

"So were you able to convince him to use his land in another way?"

"Nope. He actually had a lot of good points about opening a hotel, as much as it hurts to admit." Lydia handed Grant the curtain rod. "And he doesn't seem like he's just doing it to make money. He really wants more tourists to come to town, and it sounds like he wants to move here permanently."

Grant just nodded in response, frowning a little as he adjusted the rod into the proper place and fluffed the curtains.

"But there are already a lot of little hotels and

B&Bs and inns here—Angela and I did the research when we were looking to buy the Beachside Inn. There's only so much tourism traffic that a small island can take." Lydia stepped back to make sure the curtains looked even. "And even though the other inns and B&Bs are our competition, they still have the same energy as our place. It's all so small town and special."

"That's true. And opening on the beach will make the hotel stand out a lot." Grant came down from the ladder.

"It will! He claimed that the design would be in line with the New England style of the other buildings in the area, but there's no way to make a huge hotel have the same feel as a B&B." Lydia ran a hand through her hair. "And with huge hotels with all the amenities come more touristy things that people would expect everywhere. The Marigold-ness of Marigold would disappear, as Holly phrased it the other day."

"It would."

"The thing is, I obviously *want* people to continue to come to Marigold." Lydia slowly paced in front of the window, crossing her arms. "The town deserves to thrive. But it also deserves to have the heart that made me want to come here again and again. I see that, and so do Angela and Brooke and all our friends and family. Hunter might be charming with perfect teeth and excellent taste in home decor, but he doesn't have what we have."

Lydia stopped, feeling Grant's eyes following her back and forth. He had stopped gathering all the little screws and hardware to hang up the next set of curtains. Had he been staring at her long?

"Sorry, I didn't realize I was ranting." Lydia flushed. "Holly, Angela, and Brooke already heard this whole speech before, so speaking to a new audience has fired me up all over again."

In response, he set the hardware he'd been holding on the windowsill and stepped closer to her. He smelled like the woods, fresh and green. It was a contrast to the ocean air, but the scents blended together enticingly.

"It's fine, Lydia. I don't see it as ranting." He held her gaze, a small smile spreading across his face. His voice was soft and low. "I like how passionate you are about this. And how much you care about the inn and all its details."

Being this close to him made her heart flutter, especially since he hadn't broken eye contact. The light falling through the window caught the brown of his eyes and highlighted the little lighter flecks in them, making them seem warmer than usual.

"You care too," Lydia said, glancing down at the floor for a moment so she could catch her breath.

"I do, but not like you do."

"Is that why you withdrew your bid on the inn?" Lydia's voice lowered, almost to a whisper. "Or I guess I should first ask—did you really withdraw your bid on the inn?"

Grant paused, a flicker of doubt coming into his eyes for a second before he nodded. "Yes, I did."

"Why? You seemed so set on tearing it down and putting up something that Hunter would probably want for the island." Lydia's pulse picked up even more, a shiver going down her spine as he touched a bit of hair that had fallen into her face. He tucked it back behind her ear.

"You were just as passionate about the inn that day as you are now," Grant murmured. "After we spoke, I realized that you deserved the space. It wasn't just an investment or a project—it was a dream, and I wanted you to achieve it." He slid a rough hand down her cheek. "And I don't think I saw it that way at the time, but you stayed in my mind. I don't think I wanted you to leave."

He leaned down and kissed her softly on the lips.

It was gentle, but it made Lydia's legs feel weak, like she'd just run a marathon in thirty seconds flat. She looked up into his eyes again, seeing the softness that only she got to see regularly.

If someone had told Lydia months ago that she would be standing here in the inn that she owned, kissing Grant of all men, she wouldn't have believed it. Honestly, she probably would have laughed. She wouldn't have believed she'd ever feel like this again either, or that she would find this feeling in such an unexpected person.

But now, after months of conversations about anything and everything, of sharing their grief and connecting at a deep level, it felt right. Butterflies flapped in her stomach as her heart slammed against her ribs—she was just as terrified as she was thrilled.

But it was a *good* kind of scary.

Grant leaned in and kissed her again, just as sweetly as the first time, and a rare broad smile crossed his face when they broke apart.

"We should finish hanging these curtains," he said, squeezing her shoulder. "It'll be dinner time soon, and I'm sure Angela will be happy to see these up."

"Right." Lydia touched her lips for a moment

before she reached for the hardware Grant had set aside.

They returned to their task, shooting each other smiles and letting their hands brush against each other just a little longer than necessary as they worked.

Patrick had never realized how much stuff in their house belonged to Aubrey until it was all packed up into boxes and whisked away. Most of the smaller touches that he hardly noticed from day to day—mirrors, vases, little side tables where Aubrey put fresh-cut flowers—were gone, as were a lot of pieces of cookware that he rarely used himself.

Most of the big furniture remained, but the house still felt echoey and empty. It reminded him of the apartment he'd shared with a roommate back in college, one of the few periods in his adult life when he hadn't lived with Aubrey. The only difference was that this home was clean and had furniture that he hadn't dragged in from a yard sale.

Aubrey came down the stairs carrying a suitcase, her phone wedged between her shoulder and her ear. Patrick grabbed the bag from her, and she mouthed a "thank you." He put the suitcase next to the few others in the front entryway. Nearly all of her things were in her new apartment in Boston already.

"Yes, thank you..." Aubrey tucked a hand into her back pocket and walked slowly across the living room. "Ten is perfect..."

Patrick leaned against the couch. Now that he was seeing the excited gleam in her eyes, he wondered how he hadn't noticed her lack of spark in the past few years. She'd off-handedly mentioned moving back to Boston, where they'd both gone to college, and now she was finally doing it.

She had job interviews lined up, ones that would take her career to the next level, and she would get the excitement that she craved. She loved going to new restaurants, seeing plays, and living life at a faster pace. It had been fun for both of them when they were freshly out of school with their first adult paychecks, but it had gotten old for Patrick fast. Aubrey had loved Marigold as much as Patrick did at first, but now he could see that it just wasn't the right fit for her. To her, it was a vacation spot. To him, it was home.

Since Patrick could have lived the rest of his life in Marigold, easily, and Aubrey was miserable there, it wouldn't have been fair to try to keep their marriage together. They loved each other, but Patrick knew they would be better off—and much happier—if they could follow their own paths.

But that still didn't make the split hurt any less, even if it was for the best.

"Thanks again. Goodbye." Aubrey ended her call and put her phone into her jeans pocket.

"Was that another interview?" Patrick asked.

"Yeah. It's on Tuesday at ten." She turned toward him, her eyes softening from their excitement into what looked like worry.

"You'll do great." And he wasn't just saying that because it was polite. He knew Aubrey was great at her job, and he would always care about her well-being, even after they split up.

"Thank you." She smiled a little, even though it didn't fully reach her eyes.

She opened her arms and Patrick stepped into them, holding her. The hug reminded him that things were going to be strange without her in so many little ways. He wouldn't smell her favorite perfume or body wash in the bathroom anymore. He wouldn't hear her shuffling around in her slippers on a cold morning. He wouldn't get to just hug her like this.

"I hope you have an amazing life and career, Aubrey," he said into her hair. "I hope I can be a small part of it."

"Of course. I always want to be your friend." She squeezed him a little tighter. "Maybe your publicist will send you to Boston for your next book tour and we could get dinner or something."

"Hah, if I ever finish the book." He rubbed her upper back.

"You'll finish it. You always do, and it'll be great," she said as her phone buzzed in her pocket. "I think that's my cab."

They let go of each other, their hands lingering on each other's shoulders. Aubrey gave him a light kiss on the lips, the last one they'd ever share, and squeezed his shoulders.

He helped her carry her things out to the cab and tucked them into the trunk. She hopped into the backseat and waved as they pulled away. Patrick watched the car until it disappeared around the corner, his vision blurring a little from tears.

He blinked them away and went back inside his empty, quiet house. They lived a moderate distance from the main road and from their neighbors, their house surrounded by trees on all sides with a sliver of a view of the water. Patrick welcomed the silence when he was in the middle of writing, but now it felt different. Final, almost.

But to his surprise, the quiet didn't feel as lonely as it had while Aubrey was away in Connecticut. His marriage was over, completely. He didn't have to worry about what was happening in their relationship the moment he woke up. He didn't have to think about when Aubrey would be coming home or sit silently next to her as they ate dinner in front of the TV.

He could focus on his own life, and she could focus on hers. They didn't have to pour their energy into trying to make their failing marriage work. Instead, they could use that time to find real happiness.

Patrick's mind felt clearer than it had in a while, even though sadness still lingered in the edges of his thoughts. He grabbed a cup of tea and headed upstairs to make the most of his clear head. He had a book to finish.

CHAPTER TWENTY-ONE

During the process of renovating the inn, Angela had gotten used to hectic days and talking to people from morning to evening, whether it was contractors or antique suppliers or Lydia. The week running up to the zoning board meeting had kicked all of that into overdrive.

With Millie's help, Angela and Lydia had reached out to as many members of the community as possible to build a case against rezoning the land Hunter had purchased. Angela had spoken to everyone from the mayor's cousin to young families to some of Travis's fellow cops, trying to find anyone who would be willing to speak up against the rezoning.

Some people were won over to their side right

away, especially those who had lived on the island for a long time. They couldn't imagine Marigold changing into a more touristy town like so many others in the region, and they promised to speak up at the meeting. A few of the younger residents were harder to convince. Some of them liked the idea of a busier, more metropolitan feel on Marigold. Angela could understand that, in a way, but she thought she made her case well as to why the hotel could end up causing more problems than solutions.

Angela and Lydia had worked on their argument every single day, and now they had it down pat. There wasn't much else they could do to prepare in the short hour before the meeting.

Angela took a deep breath as she smoothed her hair into a bun. Jake was playing with some toy cars in the living room of the innkeeper's residence, and she looked over her shoulder at him.

"You ready to go hang out with Dad, Jake?" she asked, grabbing her purse.

"Yep!" Her son ran over to put on his sneakers. He got them on and mostly tied them correctly, then Angela grabbed his small backpack filled with books and other activities.

They drove over to the bed-and-breakfast across town where Scott was staying and knocked on the front door. The owner, Sandy Hawkins, let them up to Scott's room, where he was typing away on his laptop at a tiny desk in the corner. He was working remotely, which he was used to, but this space was much, much tinier than his office back home. He looked a little squished, but he didn't seem bothered by it.

"Oh, hey, buddy!" Scott said over his shoulder as he finished typing something. "Hey, Angela."

"Hey." Angela helped Jake take off his backpack and put it next to the door. "You're sure you have time to watch him?"

"Yeah, I do. I've got a few things going on, but that doesn't mean we can't have some fun." He ruffled Jake's hair.

"Okay. I'll come back to pick him up in a couple of hours. I'll text you."

"All right. Good luck."

"Thanks." She hoped they wouldn't need too much of it to win.

Angela drove over to Brooke's apartment, where she found her sister standing outside. Angela had gotten used to seeing Brooke in leggings or worn jeans and a t-shirt, covered in flour and sugar, so seeing her in a rose pink pencil skirt and cream blouse was a surprise. Her pale blonde hair was half pinned up and half around her shoulders, and she was wearing just a touch of makeup. She looked like a young professional that everyone would take seriously.

"You look great, Brooke!" Angela said as her sister climbed into the car.

"Thanks! It's nothing. All of this stuff is pretty cozy, honestly." Brooke buckled her seatbelt and put her purse between her feet. "I just wanted to look nice. It's kind of like speaking without speaking, you know?"

"Yeah, I get that."

"I just want the inn to succeed." Brooke flipped down the visor and wiped a smudge of lip gloss away. "Not wearing shorts or leggings for a few hours won't kill me."

"I think we have a strong case." Angela pulled onto the main road toward town hall, taking another deep breath through her nose. She was glad she'd spent all that money on yoga classes back in Philadelphia—she had been taking more calming breaths today than she had in months.

"We do. But we aren't world famous movie stars with a ton of cash to spare." Brooke looked out the window. "It's hard to tell what will happen."

"All we can do is our best." Angela gave the

steering wheel a squeeze. "And we have a lot of local people on our side, so that matters."

"True." Brooke fiddled with the ends of her hair. "I just can't imagine losing literally everything because of something like this."

"Hey, not everything will be lost." Angela slowed to a stop at a light. "Even if they rezone and Hunter builds the hotel, your bakery dreams won't go down with the inn."

Brooke hesitated. "I know. It just feels like the inn is a great first step. It's not like I'm diving in headfirst—it's just a toe in the water. The volume wouldn't be as nuts as opening an entire bakery, and I can see if I like it."

"It is, but it's not the only step you can take. There's the farmer's market, and there are cafes in town that could stock your pastries." Angela glanced over at Brooke. "Just think about it."

Brooke nodded, looking back out the window. Angela knew that her younger sister could do it—she just wondered when Brooke would figure that out about herself.

* * *

Lydia waved at Brooke and Angela as they walked through City Hall's parking lot. Even from a distance, she could see the nervous energy radiating between the two sisters. It was the same anxiousness she felt buzzing inside her own chest. Millie had been the only person keeping her sane and steady all day. Where Millie got the patience to deal with her worried babble, Lydia didn't know. But she was really grateful for the support.

"It looks like a full house," Angela said, looking at the parking lot. "Either that, or people are using the lot and going somewhere else."

Lydia looked over her shoulder at the building, which had its heavy wooden doors propped open. People were lingering outside the front, talking and drinking from little Styrofoam cups of tea or coffee.

"No, I think it's all for this meeting." Lydia nodded her head toward the door. "Okay. Let's do it."

They walked in together, and Lydia quickly found that she'd been right. There was a great turnout, with most of the seats filled—a great sign. She spotted Grant near the front, feeling her heart flutter the way it had after their kisses when they were putting up the curtains. He smiled back and gave her a little wave.

They found seats at the front, but neither she nor Angela were calm enough to sit still. So after reserving their seats by leaving something on the chairs, they stood and surveyed the crowd. Most people's gazes lingered on Hunter, who was talking to someone on the opposite side of the room. He looked like the star he was. His clothes, even though they weren't flashy, were clearly more expensive than what most Marigold residents were wearing, and everyone around him seemed to be hanging on his every word.

A cluster of women stood nearby, trying and failing to be subtle as they stared at Hunter. Lydia's chest tightened a little. Had people come just because of him? Surely at least one or two had, but were there enough to sway the board? Lydia could feel Hunter's charisma across the room and knew she couldn't match it. She hoped he wouldn't win everyone over with a few smiles and easy jokes.

"Hello, everyone." Marcus Trettel, the president of the zoning board, stepped up to the mic at the podium. "We should go ahead and get started."

Lydia hadn't known her heart could feel like it was literally about to punch through her chest, but that was exactly how she felt at the moment. She could hardly take in the introductory words from Marcus.

Millie nudged her when the zoning board president called for her to speak, giving her a thumbs up.

Smoothing her skirt, Lydia walked up to the podium with her sheet of notes. Some of her nervousness eased as she saw so many the people she had talked to over the past week in the audience. A lot of people supported their efforts and had taken time out of their evenings to come to this meeting. She could do this.

"My parents first brought me to Marigold when I was seven years old," she said when she reached the podium. "I remember running around on the beach with them, walking down Main Street with my aunt Millie, whom many of you know, and trying my first lobster roll by the water. I met some lifelong friends too—girls I came to know as sisters over every summer trip until I graduated from high school. It was the kind of childhood magic that many more people deserve."

As she spoke, Lydia looked out at the crowd, catching sight of Angela nodding along with her words.

"Even as I moved on in my life and lived in

various places, part of my heart felt that Marigold was home. Nowhere else is like it. While it has restaurants and stores that could rival the big city businesses in quality, it still feels like a place where everyone knows each other and can lean on each other. It's not something that you can create—it's something that's been built year after year."

She smiled as she looked out over the sea of faces before her. She had gotten to know more people during her short time in Marigold than she had ever known in her neighborhood back in Philadelphia.

"We have a lot of tourists, and we welcome them, especially every summer. But part of the reason why they come is to experience the small town charm that's rapidly disappearing from so many places." Lydia took a moment to clear her throat. The room was dead silent, everyone listening intently to her words. "Rezoning the property along the waterfront to build a large hotel might bring in more tourists, but it would also fundamentally change the feel of the island."

A few more heads were nodding in the crowd, and Lydia felt a little bubble of hope swell in her chest as she continued, delving into all the research and statistics she and Angela had put together over the past week, laying out their case as clearly as she could.

"My business partner, Angela Collins, and I— along with many of the Marigold residents in attendance—would like the zoning board to vote no on rezoning the waterfront property," she concluded. "Building a large hotel there would be the first step in transforming Marigold into yet another tourist trap and it would take away the uniqueness of what brings people here today. Thank you."

With that, Lydia folded up her paper and stepped away from the podium.

A few people clapped quietly, which made her feel like she'd done a good job. People were nodding, too, whispering to each other. Angela and Millie gave her hands a squeeze when she made it back to her seat.

"Thank you for that perspective. Now, to speak in favor of the rezoning is Hunter Reed." Marcus ushered Hunter forward, giving him space to step up to the podium.

"Thank you," the well-dressed actor said with a smile before glancing at Lydia. "And thank you for your views and your passion on this issue. I haven't lived in Marigold nearly as long as many people here —I've only just settled into my new home. But I moved here because I love it. I love the pace, I love the views, I love the food. I especially love the people."

A woman behind Lydia let out a gentle sigh, as if Hunter was speaking directly to her when he said he loved the people.

"It's a great place to be, and I want more people to come experience it. If the property along with waterfront is rezoned to allow a hotel to be built, we can create even more abundance for Marigold." He gently rested his hand on the podium. "The hotel will create jobs, and more money will flow into local businesses. It'll be different, definitely something new for the island. But it could be a *good* kind of new. The hotel will have a similar aesthetic to the other inns in town, but it'll have amenities that visitors have come to expect. It'll make Marigold more competitive with other nearby towns."

Lydia bit her lip, resisting the urge to glance around and see if people were receiving his argument well. His charisma was palpable, and his arguments were still solid. He was a good actor, of course, but it was easy to see that he wasn't just putting on a show for everyone. He meant every word.

"I moved to Marigold because of what kind of

place it is. I'd like to rezone the waterfront property so that more people can come to love this island the way I've fallen in love with it. Thank you."

People clapped for Hunter as well, nearly as hard as they'd clapped for Lydia. He took a seat on the other side in the front row.

"Thank you, Mr. Reed. Now we'll open up the floor to other members of the community to speak as to whether they're for or against the rezoning." Marcus gestured to his right. "Please form a line here and keep comments relatively brief."

Many people got into the line, several of whom had spoken with Lydia about stopping the rezoning. There was an even mix of people who were for the rezoning and people who were against it. Many of them reiterated points that Lydia had made, talking about the reasons they'd moved to Marigold, and others really seemed as if they wanted Marigold to become like every other town.

"We can take one more person. Come on up, sir," Marcus said.

Grant stepped up to the microphone, briefly catching Lydia's eye. He gave her a nod and cleared his throat.

"Hello, I'm Grant Hamlin." He glanced at Lydia again before looking into the crowd. "A few months ago, I might have been all for a big hotel on the island. I was going to buy the inn that Lydia and Angela now own—I put a bid in for it. I was going to clear the land, bulldozing the inn and replacing it with something commercial, like offices or something along those lines. Things you can find anywhere. But now, I can't imagine losing the Beachside Inn."

He paused, seeming to gather his thoughts.

"Many of you knew my late wife Annie and know that I've been grieving her absence. I think my idea of buying the inn and getting rid of it was my way of grieving. When we first arrived on Marigold Island, we stayed at the inn while we waited for our house to be finished. It was only a few weeks, but I have a lot of great memories of it—waking up to the sound of the waves, being able to walk down the beach a bit to great seafood places. They were, and still *are,* the kinds of places where the owner will come and have a chat with you, where you'll get to know the locals during your stay."

The whole room had gone silent as Grant spoke. Lydia knew that he was well known around town, and also that his reputation on the island was the complete opposite of what he was doing now. He wasn't super talkative and often seemed a little grumpy or gruff.

The man up at the podium? *That* was the Grant that Lydia had come to know, a man with a good heart underneath his rough exterior, and now everyone else got to see him, too.

"I wanted to tear down the inn because those memories hurt, and I didn't know what to do with them. I still live close by, and I used to look away whenever I passed it because it was like a stab in the heart each time. But as I got to know Lydia and Angela and heard about all their memories of the place, I realized I couldn't take away the chance for others to have those cherished moments in the future. It wouldn't be fair and wouldn't make my grieving any easier."

Lydia's lower lip wobbled a little. Grant was speaking from the heart, his words earnest and sincere, and although he was addressing the entire crowd, he might as well have been speaking directly to her.

"What draws people to Marigold is the fact that it's the kind of place where an inn can feel like a home away from home," he continued. "It's remained a close-knit place, year after year. It's up to us to preserve that and keep that feeling going for decades to come. We can't do that by building big hotels or overdeveloping the island. We can only preserve it by fostering our small businesses and communities, by embracing what makes our small town special and unique. Thank you."

Grant stepped away from the podium, and a lot of people clapped. The crowd erupted into quiet, but upbeat conversations until the zoning board president stepped back behind the podium. Lydia smiled at Grant, sneaking a glance at the zoning board members who were seated at a long table at the front of the room.

"Thank you," Marcus said. "The perspectives and arguments put forward tonight have been very illuminating. Please allow the board to discuss this privately. We'll reconvene in several minutes with our decision."

Lydia let out a long, slow breath as the council members disappeared into a conference room down the hall. They'd done everything they could. She chatted with Angela, Millie, and Brooke, although all of them were too nervous to focus on anything but their nerves.

In a few short minutes, the zoning board returned, and people settled in again.

"Thank you to everyone in attendance. The zoning board has chosen to deny Mr. Reed's request to rezone the waterfront property," Marcus said.

Lydia didn't hear much else because Brooke let out a little shriek of excitement and a good portion of the people in attendance erupted into cheers. Lydia gave Angela, then Millie and Brooke, big hugs.

"Is this really happening?" Brooke asked, breaking their hug. Her blue eyes shimmered with excited tears.

"It really is. I'm beyond relieved." Lydia ran a hand over her face and let herself take in the rest of the room.

Many people were clearly just as happy as they were. She caught Hunter's gaze across the room, and he gave her a gracious nod and a smile. He might have lived in LA and dealt with the breakneck pace of Hollywood for years, but that hadn't changed him into a sore loser.

As the meeting broke up, the crowd started to file out into the early evening air.

"Hey, I'll meet you at the car," Lydia said to Millie. "I need to talk to someone."

"Okay, no rush."

Lydia looked over her shoulder, scanning the crowd for the face she was looking for. She finally found Grant toward the back of the room, and they made their way to each other. Just seeing him at the City Hall, knowing he'd gone out of his way to reveal such a soft side of himself for the sake of the town, made Lydia's heart warm in ways it hadn't in a long time.

"I didn't know that was why you wanted to tear down the inn," she said quietly when they reached each other. "Now it makes total sense. I wouldn't be able to stand seeing a place where I'd made so many great memories with Paul every single day."

Grant put his hands into his pockets and shrugged. "I promised Annie that I would move on, and I thought that pulling down the inn would take care of it. I was struggling for a long, long time and felt like trying to move forward was impossible."

"I know that feeling well."

"It's tough, isn't it? But I just had to find new memories and perfect moments to fit in with the ones I had before. Trying and failing to destroy the past over and over again taught me that you don't have to get rid of old memories to make room for new ones."

Lydia smiled, stepping a little closer to him. "You've really got a way with words, Mr. Hamlin, you know that?"

"Only because you bring it out in me."

They kissed, their fingers lacing together between them. Lydia ran a thumb along his work-roughened knuckles, savoring the way Grant made her feel. Between the feelings building between them and her relief at hearing the zoning board's decision, she felt like she could float away with happiness.

It was the perfect end to a wonderful evening.

CHAPTER TWENTY-TWO

"Where did my checklist go? I swear it was right here," Angela said, turning around in the entryway to the inn. The plush rug that she'd managed to find felt great under her bare feet, but she couldn't focus on that—she felt three hours behind schedule.

"It's right there," Lydia said, pointing to a shelf.

"Thanks. This thing is my lifeline." Angela grabbed it and scanned the list, which Lydia had drawn up. "There's too much going on."

The two weeks after the city council denied Hunter's request to rezone the waterfront land had flown by in a flurry of last minute touches to the decor and the business side of things. Their website was up and running, as was the online booking—they already had a few reservations, including some for this evening.

Tonight was the inn's grand opening reception. On top of making sure the inn itself was in perfect condition, they also had to prepare the common space for everyone coming to the reception.

There was so much chaos with everyone running around that Angela hardly heard the knocking on the front door until she happened to rush by it.

It was the florist, finally. Angela let her in and showed her where she needed to go.

"Oh great, the flowers are here!" Lydia said, appearing behind Angela. "What about the people delivering linens?"

"They're here too—they're steaming them." Angela glanced through her list. "It looks like things are mostly on schedule."

"Maybe for a moment." Lydia adjusted her ponytail and looked at all the activity around them. "Would you mind checking in on everyone else? I'll help the florist."

"Sure thing."

Angela found a pen in a drawer and walked through the house to check off what everyone else was doing.

Brooke was arranging the mini tarts, brownies,

and cookies she'd baked on platters in the kitchen, which had become her home base. Millie was going to pick up the non-dessert food that they'd ordered after she finished with decorating the front desk. Angela's parents were scanning the rooms for any small details that others might have overlooked. Grant had the final details of the landscaping along the path to the inn under control.

Even Scott was helping with whatever was left, though he kept going to check his work email from time to time. It was an old habit that he'd had throughout their marriage. Yet he still couldn't break it, despite his attempts to do better. Angela sighed. He was still getting things done, so she moved on.

After making a lap around the inn, Angela returned to the front desk to check if they'd gotten any emails from guests. Scott's phone was there next to the computer, where he had been keeping tabs on the social media posts that they'd sent out to generate buzz.

She plopped down into the seat, rubbing her lower back, and jiggled the computer mouse to wake up the screen. If she was going to get off her feet for the first time all day, she wanted to continue doing something productive as she did.

She read over the social media responses, which

were all positive. Were more people going to show up to the opening reception than they'd expected? That would be good, but what if they ran out of food and space?

Scott's phone buzzed next to her, and she glanced at it on reflex. It was a text from a woman named Tina Oscar. Angela frowned, searching her memory for where she recognized the name from. Then it clicked—she'd met Tina at Scott's company's holiday party the year before. She was a little younger than the two of them, very pretty, and if Angela remembered correctly, not in Scott's department anymore.

The text on the lock screen read: *Hey* <3

Angela watched as the phone buzzed again with another message, and her curiosity got the better of her. She knew Scott's phone password was Jake's birthday, although it occurred to her that he might have changed it after she'd caught him cheating on her. But when she tapped the code onto the screen's keypad, it worked.

Angela checked the other texts, her stomach turning. The messages definitely weren't work related.

She stared at the phone for a few moments. It felt like her life in Philadelphia happened a million years ago, but the disbelief and shock of learning about Scott's infidelity came rushing back as if it was waiting around the corner for her to find it again. Back then, she'd known she needed time to figure out what she wanted to do. Now, her next step settled in her gut almost right away.

She took Scott's phone and walked around the inn until she found him. He was in the kitchen, holding a case of small bottles of water. Brooke was nowhere to be seen, fortunately.

Scott had a smile in his eyes when he first looked at Angela, but it turned to confusion when he took in her expression. She held up his phone. "Can we talk about this?"

She gestured toward the walk-in pantry, one of the few places where she knew they could get some privacy.

Scott followed her inside and shut the door.

"What's up?" he asked.

"What are these texts, Scott?" Angela handed him his phone.

Scott grabbed the phone and frowned. "Why were you looking at my texts in the first place?"

"Your lock screen still displays the contents of your texts, and the first one was from a woman saying 'hey' with a heart emoji." Angela crossed her arms. "It was sitting on the desk."

Scott scrolled a little, rocking back on one heel as if he was distancing himself from her. He chewed the inside of his lip, a flush of pink creeping up his neck.

"It's nothing. It wasn't like I was texting her back," he said, holding up the screen. "Look at these previous texts. I didn't respond to them."

Angela looked at the past texts, which were more flirty come-ons, asking how he was doing or telling him he had looked good that day. And he hadn't responded. But still, that didn't matter. Text messages weren't the only way two people could communicate.

"But the texts are still there," she insisted. "And there are so many of them, Scott."

"I can't control what another woman does," he said, his voice filled with frustration and defensiveness. "We haven't hooked up or anything, so I don't know where she's getting the idea to send all these texts."

"Do you not see her in person at the office?"

"I mean, sure, but that's literally it. We don't even go to lunch together." Scott stuffed his phone into his back pocket and crossed his arms over his chest, mirroring Angela. "Nothing happened, and nothing will happen. I can't stop a woman from making a pass at me."

Angela blinked, trying to wrap her head around his logic. "That's not entirely true, Scott. You can't *make* her stop, but you could have tried to tell her to stop, period. Or that you're married. Or that you're not interested. Did you do any of those things?"

Scott leaned against the shelves, his hands dropping into his pockets. "No. I didn't. But a lot has been going on at work anyway."

"It takes two seconds to send a text."

Angela studied her husband, who now couldn't meet her gaze. He looked ashamed and embarrassed, like he wanted the floor to swallow him up.

"Angela, I promise you that the affair was a one-time thing. I'll never act on anything like this again. And I'll tell her to back off." Scott finally looked back into her eyes. "I swear. I'll do better."

Angela studied Scott's face. Months ago, she would have seen his words as sincere. But they didn't matter at the end of the day. Even if he were telling the truth, she couldn't trust him on his word anymore. Back in Philly, before she'd learned of his infidelity, she had gone out of her way to make space in their schedules to have one-on-one time, to spend time with him and give him what she thought was good for their marriage. But she realized it wasn't enough—Scott just wanted and needed attention that she wasn't able to give him on her own. He would always be chasing the high of fresh attraction, the forbidden thrill of what was new.

She couldn't keep pretending that he would change. She had already given him one chance, and he'd blown it.

"I can't do this anymore," she said, her jaw tightening. "I'm done. This is over for good."

Scott ran a hand through his hair, looking down at the floor. He let out a long breath and nodded, absorbing her words.

"Okay. I understand." He opened his mouth like he might argue again or ask her to give him yet another chance, but something in her expression must've convinced him it wouldn't work. He swallowed and stepped toward the door. "I'll leave. I don't want to ruin your big opening."

"That's probably best." Angela's voice was thick with emotion, but she kept her tone firm.

Scott hesitated before he reached the door. He turned back to look at her, his expression serious. "I'd still like to be in Jake's life. Is that something you're okay with?"

"Of course." Angela softened a tiny bit, but not enough to change her mind on their marriage. "He loves you. And I want our son to have both of his parents in his life. We can discuss custody and make arrangements when we finalize the divorce."

Scott nodded again, then stepped out of the pantry, leaving Angela alone inside. She sank down and sat on a small work stool, her eyes filling with tears. It was finally over.

CHAPTER TWENTY-THREE

Lydia opened the door to the walk-in pantry expecting to find bottles of water, not Angela sitting on a crate and wiping tears from her eyes. She immediately put down the to-do list in her hand, focusing on her friend. There was still a lot to be done, but Angela's distress was the priority.

"Hey. What's wrong?" Lydia sat down on the crate next to Angela and rubbed her back.

"It's just Scott. It's over for real now." Angela sighed and dabbed at her eyes with a paper napkin she'd found somewhere. "I was sitting at the front desk going over the website and saw his phone. Some coworker of his was texting him."

"Oh no, again?" Lydia tried to remember where Scott was, just to avoid running into him. If she did, she wasn't sure if she could stop herself from giving him a piece of her mind and defending her friend.

"No, no, not like that. They never did anything." Angela blew her nose. "But she was texting him, openly flirting, and he didn't tell her to stop."

"As if that makes it any better. Ugh."

"Right? He gave me the same line about doing better and the affair being a one-time thing, but I'm not buying it. If I hadn't found out about the texts when I did, who's to say things wouldn't have progressed from texts to calls or even more? I can't live like that, constantly questioning whether he's being honest with me or hiding something. Constantly feeling like I'm not enough for him, like he'll always need more. I told him all of that. He's finally accepted that it's over, and he's gone."

Angela let her head fall back against the shelves. Then she grimaced, straightening again quickly. "Oh no, that means we'll be spread even thinner. What were his duties? Do you have your list? He was carrying all that heavy water, and I don't think anyone else could do it as quickly as he could besides Grant, but—"

"Hold up, hold up." Lydia put her hand on Angela's shoulder so she wouldn't stand up. "That can wait for a minute. You deserve a chance to breathe after everything that just happened."

Angela took a deep breath and let it out, wiping her eyes even though she wasn't crying anymore. Lydia wrapped her arms around her in a tight hug. They stayed clasped together for a while until Lydia felt like Angela was stable again.

"Thanks for that." Angela gently squeezed Lydia's forearms, then caught sight of the backs of her hands, which were smeared with mascara. "Wow, I really shouldn't have put on make-up this early."

"How would you have known you'd be crying in a pantry today?" Lydia asked. "And it doesn't look awful, really. After you rinse your face, you'll be back to normal. And besides, you've been running around all day without a break, so you wouldn't have gotten the chance to get all dolled up before anyway. At least now you can catch your breath."

"That's true. I really do need to slow down and think. This is a really big deal. I think Scott is a good father to Jake, but how will Jake be without his dad around all the time? He's really enjoyed having him here." Angela bit her lip, as if she was trying to stop herself from crying again.

"Jake has been doing well up until now, hasn't

he?" Lydia pointed out, squeezing her friend's hand. "And he has way more family support here than back in Philadelphia—his grandparents, his aunt and uncle, all of our friends. All of us love him, too. He'll never be without support."

That made Angela break into a few tears again, but happy ones. She gave Lydia another hug.

"You're right. He's been doing really well, and Scott will always be able to see him. But Jake will get to see me in a happier state of mind and get to grow up in this amazing place," Angela said. She let out a breath as they broke apart, wiping her eyes again. Then she met Lydia's gaze. "I'm so glad we ran into each other that day. And I'm really, really glad you took on this insane dream with me."

"Same here." Lydia chuckled, a combination of nerves and excitement filling her. "I can't believe the day is finally here. It feels like it took both forever and the blink of an eye to get to this point."

"That's exactly how I feel." Angela stood, dusting off her hands as a hopeful and determined expression filled her features. "Are you ready to do this?"

Lydia stood too, grinning. "As ready as I'll ever be."

* * *

Angela had dreamed of the moment when the first guests would walk into the inn, but seeing it actually happen felt surreal. She had seen clients walk into their homes or their offices after she and her team at her old interior design job redid them, and the elated looks on their faces had felt satisfying.

But this? This was a million times better.

The first guests were a middle-aged couple on a weekend trip, toting their suitcases. They looked up in wonder at the chandelier the second they stepped inside, just as Angela had intended, then around at the open entryway.

She and Lydia hadn't made a lot of changes to the layout of the inn, except for here—they'd taken down one small wall, which made a huge difference in the wow factor. Guests could see into the common space, and the lobby felt much bigger. Angela and Lydia had worked with the florist to create a beautiful summer wreath that decorated the front desk, and flower arrangements throughout the space coordinated with it.

"Hello, and welcome," Angela said from behind the front desk. "Are you here to check in?"

"We are!" The woman nodded.

"You guys are our very first guests." Angela pulled up their reservation software.

"Wow." The man looked at his wife with a smile. "That's pretty cool, huh?"

Angela smiled. It was beyond cool to her.

Their check-in went smoothly, and Angela showed them to their room. It was one of her favorites—it was ocean-themed and had a great view of the water. At this time in the evening, the walls seemed to be the same color as the sea.

"You're welcome to join us downstairs for refreshments once you've settled in," Angela said, leaving them be.

By the time she got back downstairs, even more people had arrived. Lydia was chatting with the three older women at the front of the line as she checked them in.

"Ah, there you are!" Lydia said with a smile.

"Sorry about that—I was showing our first guests to their room," Angela said.

"Don't apologize, hun," one of the women said. She had a warm southern drawl that instantly made her stand out. "We were just saying how great everything looks now that it's been renovated."

"We came here decades ago on a girls' trip," one of the woman's friends added. "It still has that charm that we loved, but it looks so much better. Lydia said that you designed it. You're very talented."

"Oh, thank you so much." Angela couldn't help but blush. That was the best compliment she could have gotten on her design work, and the evening had hardly begun. She'd been a little worried that the inn had lost some of its charm after all of her tweaks, but she thought she'd captured the feel exactly the way she'd wanted to.

Angela helped Lydia check in the group of women before showing them to their rooms. Other guests started to trickle in slowly and the small, acoustic band started playing. By the time Angela was able to snag anything to eat, the party was almost in full swing.

She loaded up her plate at the long table in the common area, her mouth watering at everything the caterer had made. She got a little of all the things she wanted to try the most—lightly fried goat cheese poppers, summer strawberry bruschetta, mini crab cakes, and baked brie and pear bites that were quickly disappearing.

Angela took a bite of the goat cheese popper first, savoring the crunch of the outside, then the melted cheese. If the rest of the appetizers were this good, she was going to end up stuffed. There was so much more food to try, but she needed to pace herself to save room for Brooke's desserts.

Her family was clustered on the side of the table housing the desserts, laughing at a joke Travis had made. Millie was drifting from group to group, saying hello to all the people she knew. Business owners Angela had gotten to know, like Cora from the butcher shop and Nicole from the art gallery, were outside, enjoying the fresh air and sipping wine.

Angela settled in a spot where she could see the front door and all the guests, just in case someone needed help. Everything was going so smoothly. The guests were talking with locals, and all of her friends and family were catching up with each other.

"Try the brie and pear bite next," Lydia said, appearing at Angela's side with a little plate of food of her own. "They're divine."

Following her friend's urging, Angela took a taste of the brie and pear appetizer. It was incredible, creamy and perfectly sweet.

"Oh man, you were not kidding." She held a hand in front of her mouth as she spoke. "I'm really glad so many people came, but at the same time, I hope there are leftovers for us."

Both women laughed, just as the energy in the

room seemed to dip. Several groups looked toward the open door, where Hunter Reed had just stepped inside. A few people turned back to their conversations, their voices low. Even though Angela and Lydia had won the rezoning battle, a lot of people in town still weren't a fan of Hunter for trying to put a huge hotel on the beach. They viewed him as an outsider who had come to their small community and tried to change things to match *his* vision of what the island should be. Angela still hadn't completely warmed up to the idea of him either.

Lydia nudged her in Hunter's direction, obviously hoping to make peace between them, and Angela let out a quiet chuckle as they headed toward the actor. She took a breath and let it out, reminding herself to be civil. After all, he had promised to be a good loser if the zoning board ruled against him. The least they could do was be gracious as well.

"Hunter, welcome!" Lydia said with a big smile.

Angela put on a smile too. "Hello."

"We're so glad you could make it." Lydia shook his hand.

"Thank you for inviting me. It looks incredible." He looked up at the chandelier before glancing from side to side to take everything in. "Congratulations on your opening."

"Thank you." Lydia put a hand on his shoulder, ushering him deeper into the inn. "Would you like some wine? The food is incredible too."

"I'd love that."

Angela followed Lydia and Hunter to the wine station, nodding along politely to their conversation when she could. Hunter eventually disappeared into the crowd as more people stepped up to Angela and Lydia to congratulate them.

They got pulled into conversation after conversation, moving around the room and checking to make sure everyone was having a good time. It felt like every single person they'd ever met in Marigold wanted to say hello and help them celebrate—Jake's friends' parents, the other female business owners Millie had introduced them to, someone Angela had gone to high school with, and even one of her old teachers.

Angela's face started to hurt from smiling and laughing so much. A while later, she excused herself to snag another one of Brooke's amazing raspberry jam filled cookies, but everyone else must've thought they were delicious too—none of them were left.

Still, having to choose a decadent mini chocolate cupcake wasn't a bad alternative.

She looked around to find Brooke to tell her that the raspberry cookies had been a hit, then paused as she spotted her across the room. Brooke was deep in conversation with Hunter, grinning up at him as she listened to him speak. Hunter must have been telling her something funny because he had a slight smile on his face too.

Angela shook her head as she turned and weaved her way back to Lydia.

Huh. Brooke and Hunter.

Were they becoming friends? Or was there more to it than that?

She wasn't sure how she felt about it, if anything was actually happening there. Hunter's charm was undeniable, and even though he seemed nice, Angela couldn't bring herself to trust him entirely when it came to her younger sister. He was still new in town, so he was probably still on his best behavior.

Angela was sure that he could have had a date every single day of the week if he wanted—he was a handsome movie star, for goodness' sake.

Brooke was stronger and more resilient than many people guessed based on her bubbly personality, and she was far from being a naïve child.

But she still tended to trust a little too easily. Angela remembered when Brooke was in high school. Her younger sister would call her to tell her about a boy she had a crush on one week, only to call again the next to sob about how he'd played with her feelings.

Angela sighed. Brooke was an adult now and didn't need her older sister meddling in her business. If something was going on, Angela would have to deal with it later. It was probably nothing.

She made a few rounds outside, listening to the band and talking with a friend she hadn't seen since high school, keeping an eye on Jake. He had gotten used to his cast and was back to running around like he always did. There were a few other kids at the party, so he had been occupied all night. She was so relieved to see that Jake had adjusted to life on Marigold so quickly. Lydia was right—he would have the support he needed here.

Something caught Jake's eye, and he peeled away from his friends, running across the yard. Angela turned and saw Patrick walking out of the inn with a glass of wine. Patrick looked surprised but pleased to see Jake's enthusiastic greeting.

There was a lightness to Patrick that Angela hadn't seen in a while. He was even a little more dressed up than she'd ever seen him. He was wearing a light blue button-down shirt and nice jeans, which was probably less comfortable than the soft t-shirts and worn jeans she was used to seeing him in.

Jake held up his cast to show off what others had drawn on it and pulled the pen that he kept in his pocket out so Patrick could sign it too. Patrick smiled, crouching down and signing the cast with a flourish.

"There we go," Patrick said, capping the marker and giving it back to Jake. "All done."

"Thank you!" Jake gave Patrick a high five and ran back to his friends, waving around his cast. "Look!"

"I'm surprised he has any space left on that thing," Angela said with a chuckle, walking up to Patrick as she tilted her head toward Jake. "He's getting as many people to sign it as he can. I've signed it twice."

"It *is* getting pretty full." Patrick stood. "I had to squeeze my name in there."

"Well, I guess it's good practice for your next book signing. How's your novel going?"

"It's good! I just sent it to my editor." Patrick's face lit up in excitement and relief. "It was a really rough start, but I think it's one of the best books I've written so far. I just had to push through those bumpy spots. And go for a lot of long walks."

"Congrats! I knew something seemed different about you—you aren't carrying that weight on your shoulders anymore."

"Yeah, definitely. Hitting send feels amazing. I always forget about that when I'm struggling to squeeze out a paragraph in the middle of the process."

"Well, I can't wait to read it."

"I'll be sure to get you a copy." He sipped his wine, looking back toward the Beachside Inn. "I should be the one congratulating you—the place looks amazing."

"Thank you. We're really happy that it's turned out this well and that so many people came. A lot of people from our high school even showed up."

"Really? Is this an impromptu reunion?" Patrick's eyes twinkled with humor.

"Goodness, no. But they did come out in surprising numbers." Angela glanced over her shoulder at the full lobby inside. "I'm glad we overestimated how much food and wine we'd need."

"Is it that obvious that I'm stuffing myself silly on those goat cheese poppers and crab cakes?" Patrick laughed. "I had to step outside so I wouldn't take the rest for myself. I could clear out everything on my own, especially after living off granola bars for the past week as I finished the book."

Angela laughed too. "You're definitely not the only one. I've made more trips to the food table than I care to admit."

"The desserts look just as incredible, but I'm trying to pace myself. Someone I talked to said your sister made them?"

"She did! She's going to be doing some baking for the inn. She's gotten so much more confident in her baking skills lately, so we're all excited for her to take this next step."

"That's great! I might get a chance to try them if I check in soon."

Angela's eyebrows went up in surprise. "What do you mean?"

"Aubrey and I are getting a divorce," he said, absently running a hand through his hair. "I'm selling the house since I don't need all that space, and I've already gotten an offer. I haven't found a new place to live, though, so I'll need a place to stay while I house hunt. The inn seems like a nice place to land."

"I'm so sorry to hear that," Angela said sincerely. She could certainly relate to the pain and resignation in his voice as she spoke. She felt the same things, even though she knew she'd made the right choice ending things with Scott.

"Thanks." Patrick gave a half-smile, dipping his chin in a nod. "It's for the best, I think. It's hard now, but I hope it'll get easier."

"I hope so, too. And you're always welcome here. A lot of the suites even have desk space and views of the ocean." Angela smiled. "Not that you'll be diving into a brand new novel right away, but it's always nice to have."

"That sounds amazing. I'll have plenty of edits to work on soon, so it'll be great to have a place to do that. Thank you." He smiled back. "If you'll excuse me, I think I'm going to grab some of those desserts before everyone else gets to them. See you around."

"See you."

Angela watched him go, making a mental note to reserve that room for him tomorrow. She knew how strangely liberating it felt to finally put an end to something so significant, but she also knew how difficult the transition was, even though Scott had technically just left hours ago.

If having a comfortable place to stay would make that transition easier for Patrick, she would be glad to have him as a guest at the Beachside Inn.

CHAPTER TWENTY-FOUR

Lydia yawned, checking her watch. It was already after eleven, and most of the guests had left. The band had wrapped up, so the atmosphere in the inn felt much quieter than it had all day. She heard the guests walking up to their rooms, quietly chatting, leaving just her closest friends and family downstairs.

Millie and Angela's parents were talking with Grant, and Brooke and Travis were sitting on the floor in the lobby with Jake, who was pushing around some circular pieces on a board. Lydia had no idea what game they were playing, but she could tell that Jake was fading quickly. The usually happy boy was starting to look a bit cranky from his fatigue. She was surprised he'd made it this late. He had been running around the entire night.

Angela came from the kitchen, nibbling on one of the few appetizers they had left. She had taken off her low-heeled sandals and replaced them with flip-flops, but still had on her party dress. Its light pink cotton was a little wrinkled but still looked great. Lydia was sure her dress had wine on it somewhere, but luckily it was navy blue.

"Is it just us left?" Angela asked.

"It is. Want to start cleaning up?" Lydia looked around.

The party guests had been respectful of the space, but it had still been a party—there were crumbs on the tables, a few stray glasses of wine that people had forgotten, and some of the decorations had been knocked askew. They could tidy up the big stuff now and do a deeper clean tomorrow.

"Yeah, we should."

Angela went to the kitchen to find some big garbage bags while Lydia grabbed some rags and other cleaning tools. Even though Lydia was moving around after being on her feet all day, she felt like she was finally decompressing from the night. No one was trying to grab her attention, and she could finally take a breath.

"That was so stressful to put together, but so much fun," Lydia told her friend as she swept crumbs into the bag Angela was holding. "My voice is probably going to be hoarse tomorrow from all the talking."

"Same here. All that running around was totally worth it, but I'm glad we won't have to plan anything that big for a while. It's all guests from here on out." Angela smiled. "A lot of people told me they were planning to send their out-of-town family here for the holidays."

"I can't even think about the holidays right now," Lydia said with a laugh. "It feels so far away but it'll probably sneak up on us before we know it."

"Probably, but it's good to know we'll have business coming in." Angela carried the bag over to another table and started dumping the food scraps into it. "We'll probably be settled into day-to-day inn owner life by then."

"Hopefully. I was talking to Cora about when she and her husband first opened the butcher shop, and she said that it felt like caring for a newborn. Late nights, constant worrying that you're ruining everything, constantly cleaning up messes." Lydia tugged apart some empty plastic cups and put them in the recycling bag.

"Ah, fun times." Angela snorted. "But hey, at least we both know that the inn won't be a newborn forever."

"And we'll probably look back on these days fondly." Lydia's face softened as she smiled.

The complete lack of sleep, diaper changes, and late-night crying jags from when Holly was a baby were still in her memory, but Holly's first giggles and the sweet smell of her hair drowned them out easily. Lydia anticipated many more sleepless nights, booking software issues, and annoyed guests, but she hoped this party would always stay at the forefront of her memories.

As a new mom, there had been some days when Lydia wondered if she would make it through, but she'd come out of the early days stronger. Now she knew she could do the same with the inn. She and Angela had plans and passion. They could take on any challenge their business threw at them. They had already gone through quite a bit.

"Mommy?" Jake appeared in the doorway with Brooke and Travis behind him. He rubbed his eyes, clearly exhausted, as were his aunt and uncle. "I'm tired."

"Let's get you to bed, sweetheart," Angela said. "It's way past your bedtime."

She quickly washed her hands and came back, picking Jake up. He was getting big, but he nestled his head in the crook of her neck with ease.

"I'll be back in a few. It shouldn't take me too long to get him settled and come back here," Angela said quietly.

"Hey, don't worry about it," Grant said, popping his head into the room from the lobby. "I can help Lydia finish up."

"You're sure?"

"I'm sure." Grant took the bag Angela had been holding before.

Millie and Angela's family followed Jake's example, heading home to sleep the party off. After a few minutes, it was just Lydia and Grant, working side by side in the easy quiet that was already a hallmark of what was between them. Having worked together on so many projects in the inn, they were able to tackle the rest of the mess quickly and efficiently. The place wasn't sparkling clean yet, but it was good enough for now. They couldn't keep their guests up with a vacuum cleaner anyway.

"Whew, my feet are killing me," Lydia said, stretching her back. She had also changed out of her fancy party shoes into flip-flops like Angela had.

They were comfortable, but they weren't the most supportive shoes in the world.

"Let's go sit on the porch for a little while." Grant nodded his head toward the front. "We haven't had the chance to enjoy that swing yet."

They went outside and settled on the comfortable porch swing that had recently been installed, gently rocking back and forth. Now that everyone was gone and the guests were settled in bed, it was truly quiet except for the sound of the waves washing ashore. They could see the ocean from their spot, illuminated by the mostly full moon. They rocked for a little while before Grant spoke.

"I have something for you. A gift."

"You do?" Lydia looked up at him, smiling. "Really?"

"Yep. Don't seem too surprised. You deserve it." He stood. "Let me grab it."

He went back into the inn and returned a moment or two later, holding a box. It wasn't huge, but it felt a little heavy when he handed it to Lydia.

"Is it a book?" she asked, tearing off the simple blue wrapping paper as Grant settled on the porch swing beside her. "It feels like a book. A big one, though. Or maybe a few of them."

"Just open it, and you'll see," he said with a low chuckle.

Lydia pulled the lid off the box, and her jaw dropped. The box was filled with framed photos that they'd found the day they sorted through the basement. The frames were beautifully made from a dark wood, etched with beautiful designs of waves and shells. Lydia's eyes got misty as she went through the pictures. He'd even included the one of her and her family.

"I built the frames myself," Grant said.

"They're so beautiful. Thank you." Lydia looked up at him, warmth spreading from her heart all the way out to her fingers and toes. "This is so incredibly thoughtful."

He just smiled, putting his arm around her. Lydia took the opportunity to kiss him on the cheek.

"I'm glad you like it." He ran his hand up and down her shoulder, letting them soak in the silence again for a few moments. "I'm glad I met you, too."

"I'm so happy I met you, Grant. I don't think this place would feel the same without you."

They gently rocked in the swing and looked out onto the water. Lydia rested her head on his shoulder, savoring his woodsy scent mixed with the ocean air and the softness of his shirt against her skin.

They didn't have to speak to enjoy each other's company—just being next to each other was enough. She understood him, and he understood her. Everything felt... right.

After a while, Grant yawned, pulling Lydia out of her reverie.

"It's getting pretty late. I should head home before I pass out on this swing." He stood and stretched a little.

"I should get some rest too." Lydia got to her feet as well.

"You need it more than I do. It's been a busy day for you." He took her hand, walking them down to the beach.

"Hey, it was just as busy for you. You've been helping from the start." They stopped once their feet hit the sand. "Goodnight. And thank you again, for everything."

"Goodnight."

Grant kissed her softly on the lips, then on the forehead, and headed down the beach toward his house. Lydia watched him walk away, still feeling the tingling warmth from his kisses. She had forgotten that sweet, giddy feeling of kissing someone new. Someone she really cared about.

Her phone suddenly buzzed in her pocket,

startling her. It was one in the morning—who could possibly be calling her?

She checked who it was and smiled.

"Hey, Hols. You startled me there for a second," Lydia said, kicking off her flip-flops and walking a little farther onto the beach. "What time is it there?"

"It's six in the morning. It's one there, right? I hope I didn't wake you."

"No, no, it's all good. The last guest just left." Lydia wondered when she would tell Holly about Grant. Now wasn't the time, but she would soon. "I should ask you why you're up so early. My daughter up at six in the morning, sounding somewhat awake? Should I be worried?"

Holly laughed. "I'm only up because I have to catch a train. I've already had two cups of coffee."

"Where are you heading?"

"To France. We're going to stop in a few little towns on our way to Paris. We'll stay there for the weekend and see all the museums and sights." Holly sounded excited. "But I called to ask about the inn's opening. How did it go?"

Lydia walked closer to the water. She was touched that her daughter had remembered, even in the middle of all her fun studying abroad.

"It was so amazing. So many people showed up,

and it seems like people are going to recommend the inn to all their friends," Lydia said. "It was packed, even in the yard. A small local band played, and everyone loved all the food and desserts."

"Did Brooke make the desserts?" Holly had fallen in love with Brooke's treats during her visit.

"Yep. They were incredible. Everyone couldn't stop raving about them, so that's a good sign now that we're officially open."

"And all the finishing touches got done?"

"Every last one. We're completely done. Our first guests are settled in their rooms too. I can't wait to show you everything now that we're up and running. It's beautiful."

"I'm so excited to see it. Congrats, Mom. This is seriously cool."

Lydia could hear the grin in Holly's voice and felt a rush of pride—for herself, and for her daughter, too. She was growing to be such a compassionate and thoughtful young woman. Lydia missed her dearly, but she knew that Holly was going to do great things.

"Thanks, sweetheart."

"I've gotta go. We're heading to the train station. Love you lots, and good luck."

"Love you, too. Be safe."

Lydia ended the call, still smiling to herself. She

looked out onto the calm waters, then glanced behind her at the inn. The moonlight reflected against the white paint of the siding, and the large building was mostly dark inside except for a few lights in the windows from the guests. Even at night, the Beachside Inn looked warm and cozy, a perfect place to truly find peace.

Looking at it from this spot made her feel both nostalgic and excited for the future. The building looked fresh, but still felt like they'd captured a snapshot of her childhood perfectly. They had poured so much love into the place, and Lydia hoped her guests would feel it. The inn had been like a second home to her growing up, and now it could feel like that for someone else, too. For *many* people. The possibilities were endless.

Lydia let the cool water of the waves rush up onto her ankles and reached into the small pocket in her dress. Paul's letter was there where she'd put it earlier in the day, folded neatly. It had been a long time since she'd read it, but she'd wanted to have it with her on this momentous night. It didn't feel quite as sad to unfold it now—it was almost bittersweet.

She read it again, and one of the last lines stood out to her as it always had.

Do something that scares you. Maybe not right away, but don't wait too long. Just trust me on this.

Lydia pressed the worn paper to her heart, thanking her husband in her head. He had known exactly what she needed, even before he was gone. Opening the inn had been terrifying, but it was also one of the most satisfying experiences of her life. Nothing could come close to seeing the looks of wonder on the guest's faces, or standing on the porch and looking out onto the water as she had when she was a little girl.

Lydia folded the note again and tucked it back in its safe spot before heading back toward the inn. She looked up at the cozy, welcoming building and couldn't help but smile.

Just as Paul had wanted, she had done something that scared her. And it was the best leap of faith she'd ever taken.

The series continues in Beachside Beginnings! Get your copy and continue your journey with the characters on Marigold Island.

ABOUT THE AUTHOR

Fiona writes sweet, feel-good contemporary women's fiction and family sagas with a bit of romance.

She hopes her characters will start to feel like old friends as you follow them on their journeys of love, family, friendship, and new beginnings. Her heartwarming storylines and charming small-town beach settings are a particular favorite of readers.

When she's not writing, she loves eating good meals with friends, trying out new recipes, and finding the perfect glass of wine to pair them with. She lives on the East Coast with her husband and their two trouble-making dogs.

Follow her on her website, Facebook, or Bookbub.

Sign up to receive her newsletter, where you'll get free books, exclusive bonus content, and info on her new releases and sales!

ALSO BY FIONA BAKER

The Marigold Island Series

The Beachside Inn

Beachside Beginnings

Beachside Promises

Beachside Secrets

Beachside Memories

Beachside Weddings